HIP HOP TALES

A BIT OF SUGAR

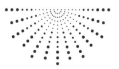

DEBBIE WILSON

Dedication

First and foremost, I want to thank my husband, James, for all the love and support he gave me through this journey. To my three wonderful children who mean the world to me. To my parents for allowing me to follow my passion for horses. A special thanks to Dr. Patricia Kusik for her encouragement; without her this dream would have never been realized.

CHAPTER ONE

M rs. Tucker, the fourth-grade teacher at Winslow Elementary School, asked everyone to pull out their copies of *Little House in the Big Woods* and follow along. As the students took turns reading, Laura Maynor became lost in her *own* story: She was riding the prettiest pony in town.

As Laura galloped up the hill, her long blond hair, wrapped in a tight ponytail, moved in harmony with the pony's tail. The countryside was filled with sunflowers at the peak of their beauty. Freshly fallen red and gold leaves lie under the majestic, mature trees. Migrating geese flew overhead in a perfect V formation. An eagle, perched in a gigantic oak, watched her every move. Laura leaned forward, urging her pony to go faster. If a grade could be given for daydreaming, she would have received an A+.

Laura had just reached the crest of the hill in her fantasy when she was startled by the teacher's firm voice.

"Laura! Laura Maynor!" Mrs. Tucker firmly said. "It's your turn to read!"

Laura tried to find her place in the book, but it was obvious to everyone that she hadn't been paying attention.

"Were you daydreaming again?" Mrs. Tucker asked loudly in front of the whole class.

Laura's face turned fire-engine red. She tried desperately not to cry as her classmates broke into heartless giggles.

Sitting at her desk, waiting for this horrible day to end, Laura chewed her nails nervously. She was anxious to go home. There was some comfort knowing that her mom was picking her up after school.

Laura slumped into her seat and slammed the car door. "Are you okay, Laura?" Laura's mom, Rose, asked with concern.

"No! It was the worst day ever! I hate school!" Laura said as she turned swiftly away from her mother, tears pouring out of her hazel-blue eyes. "I'm never going back!"

"What happened? Did those boys make fun of you again?" Rose asked, as she handed her daughter a tissue and proceeded to drive home. "Because if they did, we'll turn around and we will march right back into school and get this straightened out!"

"No, Mom. No one called me 'fat' today. I was confused when we were reading a book out loud, and when Mrs. Tucker called on me, I was lost. The whole class laughed at me."

"Were you daydreaming again, Laura? You need to pay attention in class," Rose said with concern. "You only have a week of school left before summer break."

"I tried to pay attention, but the book had ponies in it," Laura said. "And I was thinking about having one of my own."

"I know you would love to have a pony, but it's a lot of responsibility. You need to do well in school—that's your first priority. We've talked about this before, and I still don't think you're ready.

"I know, but Pop-Pop told me last week that I *am* ready and that he would help me," Laura said, as her tears stopped streaming. "I heard you and Dad fighting about getting me a pony the other night. And you're wrong! I *am* old enough! You're never, ever going to let me have one, are you?"

In the silence that followed, Rose tried to compose herself. "Laura, I'm sorry you heard us arguing, but please don't be rude to me. I will not tolerate you talking to me in that way."

"Yes, ma'am," Laura replied. "I'm sorry, but I still want a pony."

"That's enough talk about a pony, and please stop chewing your nails. I was thinking we could stop by Eugene's Store after church on Sunday and pick up ribs to take home. Doesn't that sound nice?"

Laura reluctantly nodded in agreement as she stared out the open window. The warm breeze blew across her face.

"Can you smile a little for me?" Rose asked. "Sunday is just two days away and I can't wait to spend the whole day with your dad. It will be nice having him home."

Laura rode in the backseat after the long sermon at church that Sunday. She gazed out of the car window, staring at the clouds floating by. She began to fantasize about winning the trophy at the Maryland State Fair. Pop-Pop had taken her there last year, and she had never seen anything more exciting. In her current daydream, she rode a magnificent pony with a long flaxen mane and tail. The beautiful pony performed perfectly.

When all the riders and ponies lined up in the center of the ring, waiting to hear the judges' results, all of the other riders glared at Laura and her mount with extreme envy. In her fantasy, Laura had just won the trophy, and a proud smile covered her face.

Her dad saw her smile in the rearview mirror and asked with a chuckle, "Laura, what are you thinking about?"

"Um, well, I was just thinking what it would be like to have my own pony."

Her dad laughed. "Why am I not surprised? Rose, why don't you tell Laura about the pony your dad gave you on your birthday?"

"Mom, is that the pony in the picture that you keep in your Bible along with my baby picture?"

"Yes, it is. When did you see that?" Rose asked.

"I was looking up a Bible verse for Sunday school when I saw it. Please tell me about him," Laura said, with her hands tightly gripped together.

"All right," Rose said with a deep sigh. "His name was Trigger, and Pop-Pop had a cowboy bring him to my tenth birthday party for pony rides. He was the most well-mannered pony I had ever seen. All my friends took turns riding him, and he was so patient with them. There must have been fifteen kids from the neighborhood climbing on and off him." Rose paused and wiped a tear from one of her eyes.

"What happened next?" Laura asked impatiently.

"Well, I was the last one to get on—my dad had reminded me I needed to be a good host to my friends. I remember petting his nose as he turned around and noticing his deep red color." Rose pulled a tissue from her purse and held it tightly in her hand. "His coat was as shiny as a new copper penny. When I climbed on and went for my turn around the yard, I couldn't believe how comfortable he was to ride. When the cowboy stopped Trigger, he said, "Happy Birthday, Rose! He's your birthday present from your parents!"

Rose abruptly stopped the story as a lump formed in her throat.

"Was Trigger your best birthday ever?" Laura asked intently.

"I'll finish the story another day. He was truly one of the best friends I have ever had," Rose said.

They pulled into Eugene's Restaurant as Rose carefully wiped more tears from her face and said, "I'll be right back. Can you and Laura go over to the fruit stand and pick out a nice watermelon?"

"Yes. Come on, Laura, we have an assignment," her dad said, as they stepped out of their green 1964 Buick sport wagon.

"Dad, have you heard that story before?"

"A long time ago, Mom-Mom told me about the pony."

"I was surprised to see Mom cry," Laura said.

"I've only seen her cry a couple of times," her dad shared. "When Pop-Pop had a heart attack, she was so scared he wasn't going to make it, and the stress of taking care of so many horses really took a toll on her."

Laura and John made their way back to the car. "We beat her!" John said, laughing.

The aroma of the hot ribs flooded in as the car door opened. "They smell delicious! My mouth is already watering!" John commented.

"Mine too!" Laura said. "I wish I had a best friend like Trigger."

There was no response from Rose. Laura thought, *If I had my own pony, he would be my best friend, too.*

"Laura, where would we keep a pony?" John asked.

"At Pop-Pop's of course. His barn is empty. He told me he used to have almost a hundred horses, so one pony would be fine. I would love to go to the State Fair!"

"Laura, you're right," Rose said, as she broke her silence. "He did have a lot of horses at one time, but they demanded too much of his energy. He had to sell them after his heart attack." John turned and looked at Rose and gently stroked her hand. Rose continued,

"That's why I don't want him to have to care for even one pony now. Can you understand that?"

"Yes, but I would help," Laura said, trying to assure her mother.

"I know you would, but we don't live close enough to go every day. Knowing your grandfather, he wouldn't be able to have just one pony," Rose said, shrugging her shoulders. "It took Mom-Mom and me years to talk him into selling the ones he had. It was such a sad day when they left. Pop-Pop never really seemed truly happy, until you were born. Do you remember the day he bought you the Breyer barn and horses?"

"Yes! That was awesome!" Laura said with a smile covering her face. "I still love to play with my model horses."

"He seemed like a kid again sitting in the middle of the living room making horse noises with you," Rose said. "He honestly has a deep love for horses and I think you have the same passion. We will talk about a pony maybe next year, okay? I think that's enough pony talk for today."

"Yes, ma'am," Laura said reluctantly with a sigh. She stared out the window watching the countryside go by.

The family sat down at the small four-person kitchen table to eat the delicious spareribs. They laughed as they looked at each other with their faces and fingers covered in barbecue sauce.

"What are you going to do after we clean up?" John asked Laura.

"I think I'm going to go play with my Breyer horses," Laura replied.

"Can you make your bed first?" Rose asked as she cleared the dirty dishes from the table.

Laura shook her head in agreement, washed up, and then trotted towards her bedroom. She quickly made her bed and proceeded to set up her barn with her favorite Breyer horses. The make-believe stable was very active, with model horses being shuffled from their barn to their turnout fields. Her dad could hear the whinnying sounds of her play as he passed by her room. He stopped and watched, enjoying the moment.

CHAPTER TWO

L aura and her dad played catch in the backyard
when Pop-Pop came out of the screen door.

"Jack, I didn't expect to see you today," John said,
as Laura ran and hugged her grandfather.

"Your grandmother made you cookies and dinner,"
Pop-Pop said to Laura, kissing her on the head. "Mom-
Mom finished Laura's blanket and wanted to bring it
to her. Laura, you better go grab a cookie." The two
men sat down across from each other at the rustic
wooden picnic table.

"Yeah!" Laura said as she darted into the house.

As Laura quickly grabbed a fresh chocolate chip
cookie, she overheard her grandmother and mother
talking in her bedroom. She quietly headed towards

the chatter to investigate. She stood motionless, leaning against the hallway wall, and listened intently.

"Here's Laura's blanket I fixed," Mom-Mom said, handing it to Rose. "It should be in good shape now."

"Thanks, Mom, she does love this blanket," Rose said as she meticulously spread the blanket across Laura's bed.

"I heard you're considering letting Laura take riding lessons," Mom-Mom said. "I am so happy you changed your mind."

"I'm not sure I ever had a chance," Rose said, shrugging her shoulders.

I can't believe it! Laura thought to herself. She couldn't resist the temptation of the delectable cookie and took a tiny nibble.

"I hope one day you'll allow her to have her own pony," Mom-Mom said as she readjusted her hair comb. "Watching you with Trigger are some of my favorite memories. Do you remember all the crazy things you did with him? Some days I thought you would never come in from the barn without him with you."

"Mom, I really don't want to talk about this," Rose said as she stood up and headed towards the hallway.

Oh no, Laura thought as she headed towards the back door, leaving a trail of cookie behind.

She made it to the kitchen, realizing she had only a smidge of cookie left in her hands.

"Laura," Rose said as she leaned over to pick up the pieces. "Are you in here?"

Laura headed towards the yard, holding the screen door till it shut completely and silently. She quickly ran and planted herself next to her beloved grandfather.

"What are you up to?" Pop-Pop asked Laura.

"Uh, nothing," Laura said quickly.

Rose appeared at the door and said, "Dad and John, could you come give me a hand moving a dresser in our room?"

The men reluctantly made their way in the house to help, passing Mom-Mom heading towards the picnic table to sit with Laura. She sat across from Laura and handed her another cookie.

"I think your mom found the missing pieces to your first cookie, young lady," Mom-Mom said.

"Yes, I heard you and Mom talking about a pony," Laura said.

"Well, you shouldn't be eavesdropping, but I can understand why you would be interested," Mom-Mom said. "I think it's time you know what happened to Trigger."

Laura uncrossed her pretzeled legs and sat straight up.

"Pop-Pop had fed the horses their grain and was

going to eat his breakfast while they finished theirs. He noticed the latch on the stallion door was missing a screw, and he planned on fixing it when he returned. Trigger was in the barnyard eating when Nick the stallion busted out and by the time Pop-Pop returned, it was too late. Trigger was so badly injured, all the money in the world wouldn't have helped."

Laura was startled to see her mother heading towards the table, wiping away the tears rolling down her face.

"Mom, why would you tell Laura that awful story?" Rose asked.

"I think it's time she knows why you have been so opposed to her having a pony," Mom-Mom said as Rose sat next to her. "I had never seen your dad so troubled than on that day."

"I guess I never thought how much it upset him. He went and bought me another pony the next day," Rose said, trying to hold back the tears.

Laura handed her mom the tattered napkin from her cookie. Rose half smiled as she graciously took the napkin.

"Your dad was trying to fix everything when he bought that pony. He wasn't trying to replace Trigger," Mom-Mom said, as she tightly wrapped her left arm around Rose's shoulder. "You never went down to see the new pony. Every day he took care of that sweet pony, it broke his heart."

"I just couldn't imagine going down to the barn and not hearing Trigger whinnying to me," Rose said. "I never thought about how much Dad was hurting too."

"I think it would make the whole family happy if at least Laura took riding lessons," Mom-Mom said. "What do you think Rose?"

Laura anxiously stared at her mother, waiting to hopefully hear her dreams come true. Rose reached across the wooden table and gently squeezed Laura's arm.

"I couldn't agree more!" Rose said. "Maybe Pop-Pop could call Mrs. Taylor?"

"I sure can!" Pop-Pop said with an enormous smile. "I'll call her first thing in the morning."

Laura jumped up from the table and ran over to give her mom a much-deserved hug. Rose kissed her beloved daughter on her head and couldn't hide her joy.

"We better get cooking Sunday dinner if we're going to eat before dark," Mom-Mom said as she headed towards the kitchen.

.   .   .

A fter dinner on Friday night, Laura and her dad sat side by side in the backyard on two empty upside-down buckets, preparing for the next morning's crabbing adventure. "I love being on the water early in the morning and watching the sun come up, don't you?" John asked his daughter as he finished cutting the rope. "It was a long week at work!"

"It was a long week at school, too," Laura said, as she watched her dad use the large knife.

"Yes, but you'll be finished with school soon," Dad said, tugging on Laura's arm. "Laura, I want you to tie the chicken necks on the rope about every ten feet."

"How long is the rope?" Laura asked.

"About four hundred feet from buoy to buoy. That's about average for a trout line."

"This is disgusting!" Laura said as she got a whiff of the rotting chicken necks. She crinkled her nose and turned her head away, trying not to gag. "This smells like the dead skunk we saw when we went hiking last week."

"I don't think it's that bad," John said as he laughed. "If it makes you sick, I can do it."

"No, I'm okay! I'm so excited to go crabbing. It's all I could think about this week. It's so cool you have all day Saturday off!"

"I'm excited too, it sure doesn't happen often," Dad said, as he continued tying the necks on the line.

"Does that mean that you weren't dreaming about ponies this week? I always dreamed about you becoming a commercial crabber."

"Dad, you must be kidding me," Laura said with her eyes wide open. "I'm going to be a horse trainer! These chicken necks are so slimy, I can barely hold onto them. Do you know if Pop-Pop ever heard back from Mrs. Taylor about when I can start riding lessons?"

"I haven't heard anything about that," Dad said, standing up. "You'd better go get cleaned up and get to bed. Four o'clock in the morning will be here sooner than you think. I'll finish the rest of the line."

"Why do we have to leave so early?"

"The best time to catch crabs is when the high tide is heading out, and in June, that's normally before noon," Dad said.

They were on the Chesapeake Bay promptly at 5:00 a.m. As they raced across the waves to their destination, Laura stood at the head of the bouncing boat holding a line tied to a shiny cleat. The rise and fall of the boat swept her into a daydream. She closed her eyes and felt the rhythm of jumping her champion pony over three-foot jumps all in a row. John watched Laura, and he knew she wasn't on the water anymore, but in a large meadow somewhere, riding.

That afternoon, as they returned home, Rose was waiting in the driveway. "How many did you catch?"

"Almost four dozen!" Laura said in delight. "It was a great day!"

"I'll clean the boat and then we can steam the crabs and the corn we picked up on the way home," Dad said.

"That sounds wonderful," Mom said. "There should be enough left over that I can make crab soup. I picked up some fresh vegetables at the farmer's market today."

"Mom, your crab soup is the best!" Laura said as she hugged her mother.

"Well, thank you," Rose said as she quickly backed away from her daughter. "You smell like a dead fish! Why don't you go take a shower?"

"Yes ma'am," Laura said. "Did Pop-Pop call about lessons?"

"He did, but he hasn't heard back from Mrs. Taylor yet," Mom said. "I know how excited you are, but we need to be patient. It sounds like Mrs. Taylor is very busy. Now go get in the shower.

The delicious smell of the steaming crabs overtook the house. Laura quickly got dressed and ran towards the garage to see her dad. "Are they ready?"

"Not yet," Dad said as he sat down on the bench with the paper in his hands. "They just started steaming. Do you remember how long they take now?"

"Yes, twenty-eight minutes from when they start to steam," Laura said.

"Good job, Laura," Dad said. "I already put the newspaper and the crab mallets on the picnic table, so we are ready to eat once they are done."

The piping hot crabs, with the corn mixed in, were carefully piled in the middle of the table. Melted butter for dipping the delicious crab meat was carefully placed next to Laura, with a roll of paper towels readily available.

"Laura, be careful, they're very hot," Dad said, as he sat down next to her. "Do you remember how to open them?"

"Not really," Laura said, looking up at her father.

"Flip the crab over and pull the crab's apron up, then put your thumb between the shell and the body of the crab, and pull it off," Dad said, demonstrating on his crab.

"I got it!" Laura said as the crab came apart.

"Now clean out the lungs, or the devils, but remember not to eat them, and then crack it in half." He watched Laura's progress and said, "Good job. Now let's crack those claws open. Grab a mallet and hold on to the claw. Wait, let me show you," Dad said, as he reached for the butter knife, and placed it right below the pinchers of the claw. Holding the knife steady with one hand, he used the other to hit the knife with the mallet, splitting the hard shell and exposing the juicy white meat.

"Now all you have to do is pull it out and eat," Dad said, as he handed her the exposed claw meat.

Laura took the hammer in her right hand, and with all her might, banged the claw. It flew unexpectedly through the air towards her mother.

"Watch out, Mom!"

Rose ducked as she stepped out of the back door. "That was close!"

"Sorry! I guess I hit it too hard!" Laura said, trying not to giggle.

"No problem," she said, smiling. "But we better get serious about getting these crabs picked, so I can make crab soup for tomorrow," Rose said, as she sat across from John and Laura.

"Has Pop-Pop heard back about the riding lessons?" Laura asked.

"No, not yet," Rose said. "How about I let you know when I know something? That way you won't have to ask me one hundred times a day."

"Yes, ma'am," Laura said. "But I just can't wait to ride. I sure hope it's soon."

John leaned over and kissed Laura on her head and

said, "I know it's hard to wait, but sometimes dreams require patience. How about at bedtime when you say your prayers, thank God that your mother is now okay with you taking lessons. We have to remember to be grateful for what God has already given us, before asking to receive more. It's all in His timing."

CHAPTER THREE

The Sunday sermon was shorter than usual. "We all must remember God has a plan, and we need to learn how to accept things we have no control over. We must find peace in our hearts and trust in God. Amen." And with that, Pastor Grove concluded his talk.

Laura and her parents opened their hymnals and, standing, sang "How Great Thou Art" in unison with the congregation. Laura thought to herself, *I sure hope Pastor Grove knows what he's talking about. I don't know how much longer I can wait to start riding."*

"You shouldn't race in the church parking lot," Rose called out, as John and Laura ran towards the car. "It makes it look like you can't wait to leave."

John walked quickly back towards Rose and said, "We will do our best to behave!"

"I'm not sure if that's possible. You two both act like children sometimes," Rose said as she giggled.

"Can I get a root beer when we stop to pick up ribs?" Laura asked.

"We aren't going to get ribs today," Rose said, as she opened the car door, "Remember, we are having crab soup today. I stayed up till eleven last night making it."

"Oh, that's right. I can't wait," Laura said.

The threesome headed out the curvy long drive of the church parking lot, and instead of turning left, they made a right. Laura didn't even notice, as she was daydreaming about ponies again. Ten minutes later, the car slowed down and turned into a V-shaped dirt driveway, bringing Laura out of her trance. The historical marker said "Hadley Farm." Laura's confusion turned to delight as the car drove down the dusty lane.

The trees seemed like they touched the clouds; they were so tall. Their branches shaded the entire width of the lane. Post and rail fence ran the entire length. There were lush green pastures as far as you could see, with ponies scattered throughout the fields.

"Wait, what are we doing here?" Laura anxiously asked.

"This is our stop," John happily replied.

As they made their way down the lane, Laura caught a glimpse of a familiar truck. Mom-Mom and Pop-Pop were there waiting for her. Laura jumped out of the car and ran over to see her grandparents. She tightly hugged her grandfather and said, "Thank you so much!"

"Well, you have a lesson in a half hour. Mrs. Taylor called last week, but we wanted to surprise you!" Pop-Pop said.

"Really? Oh my gosh, I can't believe it! Where do I go?" Laura asked as she scanned the area.

"Slow down, Laura, you need to change your clothes first," Rose said. "I have play clothes for you in the back of the car. Hop in the backseat and you can change out of your church clothes."

Laura changed as fast as she could and then rejoined her family. Together, they headed toward the quaint red barn. Ponies peered through the fences on both sides of the path. Laura found it difficult to keep up with her family. She couldn't stop staring at their big brown eyes gazing right back at her.

Mrs. Taylor stood by the barn with her six beloved dogs and a battered bucket in her overworked hand. Her hair was as white as snow, and her sundress seemed to dance in the breeze. Her lovely worn face seemed to reflect all her years of farm life. She was barely as tall as the fence post she was standing beside.

Pop-Pop shook Mrs. Taylor's hand and proceeded to introduce his family.

"Mrs. Taylor, I'm sure you remember Virginia, my wife, and Rose, our daughter."

"Of course. It's nice to see you again, Virginia." She stretched out her arm to shake hands. "And how could I forget one of the most talented riders I've ever met? How have you been Rose?"

"It's good to see you, Mrs. Taylor. This is my husband, John, and our daughter, Laura."

"Nice to meet you, John. Laura, I've heard so much about you. You sound so much like your mother. A true horsewoman in the making," Mrs. Taylor said as she shook John and Laura's hands.

"Yes, ma'am. I want to be a horse trainer when I grow up," Laura replied, almost speechless.

"Sounds like an ideal job for you, but we better start with the basics today. I have two very different ponies for you to ride for your lesson today," Mrs. Taylor said, resting her arm on the fence. I will meet you in the barn after I feed my stallion. My granddaughter Jodi is in the barn getting them ready. Head on in there and she will help you."

"Laura, why don't you and Pop-Pop go to the barn, and I'll show your dad around the farm with Mom-Mom," Mom said.

Pop-Pop and Laura headed one way and the rest

of the family headed down a dirt path towards well-maintained gardens. Laura and her grandfather walked into the little red barn and saw four eyes peering at them through the wooden boards of the stalls: two ponies tied in individual stalls. Laura had found her heaven. The smell of hay, grain, and ponies stopped her in her tracks.

Jodi came out of the tiny room used to store tack. She was carrying a rustic bucket filled with brushes, and she moved in a very confident way.

"Hi, I'm Jodi. You must be Laura. Here are some brushes. You can brush Pinocchio. He's the one in the stall behind you. I'll start to tack up Rags."

"Hi, Jodi, I'm Laura's granddad, Jack Anderson."

"Hello, Mr. Anderson. Do you want to wait by the ring while we get the ponies ready?" Jodi asked, with her hand on her hip.

"No, thank you. I'll stay here with Laura. This is her first time and I haven't been around ponies for a while and I've sure missed it."

"Oh, I thought you had ponies. Laura, have you never ridden before?" Jodi asked snippety.

"No, this will be my first time," Laura said, beginning to chew her nails.

"I had some ponies many years ago. Which one is Pinocchio?" Pop-Pop asked with frustration in his voice.

"He's the one right behind you," Jodi answered as she tramped into Rag's stall.

"Don't let her bother you. She's just jealous," Pop-Pop whispered in Laura's ear.

"Why is she jealous of me?" Laura quietly asked.

"I'll fill you in later. Let's get grooming. I want you to enjoy yourself today."

Laura walked into the stall, trying not to trip on the deep straw bedding. She approached Pinocchio, letting him smell her hand. She felt his warm breath blow across her hand. Laura ran her hands along his neck and down his fuzzy back.

"I've never seen a pony this color before. What do you call it?" Laura asked Pop-Pop.

"They call it silver dapple, it's kind of a mousy color. I bet after a bath his mane and tail would shine like silver. I think he's around ten and a half hands tall."

"What's a hand?" Laura asked.

"Horses and ponies are measured in hands. There are four inches to each hand, so I guess he's about forty-two inches tall."

Mrs. Taylor entered the barn. "Sorry I took so long. My poor old stallion has no teeth left. I have to soak his food for hours so he can eat it. It's tough getting old. I see you met Pinocchio. He's a good boy, just a bit green. I think Jodi has ridden him about fifteen times. Isn't that right, Jodi?"

"Yes, Gram," Jodi replied.

"He's only six, and some of these thick-headed Shetlands aren't really well broke till they are around eight, but this one is a quick learner. Have you met the other pony?" Mrs. Taylor said, walking across the aisle. "He just arrived late last week from the Eastern Shore of Maryland. His name is Hadley Ragged Robin. We call him Rags. He is twelve years old, eleven hands tall, and has an extensive show record. In fact, he has won the Maryland state trophy three times with three different girls. Laura, come into the stall with me."

"Be careful, Laura. He just nipped at me," Jodi announced.

"Jodi, tack up Pinocchio, and that's enough from you. Laura, he did no such thing. He wouldn't hurt a fly," Mrs. Taylor said, shaking her head in disgust.

"Yes ma'am," Jodi quickly replied. She rolled her eyes as she headed into the tack room.

"Come on, Laura," Pop-Pop encouraged her. "He looks very sweet."

Rags was a deep red chestnut, with a white blaze that ran down the middle of his dished face. His long mane matched his blaze, almost touching his nose. His tail dragged on the ground, which gave him a royal appearance. Rags knew he was special, having always had his own girl who cared for and loved him.

Laura walked into the stall, but instead of examining him as she did Pinocchio, she hesitated after the report Jodi had given. Soon, she realized how agreeable he was. She hugged him, wrapping her arms tightly around his neck and burying her nose into his mane. It was the most soothing scent she had ever smelled.

Pop-Pop walked into the stall to take a closer look. He moved his hands all over Rags, checking for any lumps or bumps that could cause an issue.

Rose and Mom-Mom arrived at the barn just in time to see Laura in the stall hugging Rags. They looked at each other in delight, curious if this pony could possibly be Laura's new pony.

"They remind me of how you looked the day you got Trigger," Mom-Mom said to Rose. "It was one of the most memorable days of my life."

"Would you like to take Rags for a walk while Jodi finishes up?" Mrs. Taylor asked Laura. Jodi walked by glaring at Laura.

"Yes!" Laura said in delight.

Mrs. Taylor showed Laura the correct way to lead a pony. "You always want the pony on your right side. Hold your right hand close to the halter, with the extra lead rope in your left hand. Make sure you never wrap the lead rope around your hand."

"Like this?" Laura asked as she walked towards the large maple tree.

"Yes, that's perfect," Mrs. Taylor replied.

"Is he for sale?" Laura asked upon her return.

"Laura," Dad abruptly said. "I'm not sure if your mother is ready for that yet."

"It's okay, John," Mom said. "I don't think we could fool her for long that we've already agreed to possibly purchase her a pony. I've accepted the fact that Laura's passion for horses isn't going away. So, Laura, yes, he is for sale, both ponies are, and today you're going to ride both of them to see which one is the most suitable for you."

Mrs. Taylor said, "Don't mean to interrupt, but Rags is one of the best ponies I have ever bred. He has been owned by three different girls, all of whom have outgrown him. Each time he comes back to sell to the next child. All my ponies are sold with a contract, and in the contract, the owner must notify me when they are going to sell the pony. This ensures the pony's best interests are taken care of, assuring they never end up in an auction or a bad situation. Rags is so special that I insist he comes back to my farm to be sold, and I personally meet the buyers."

"I would never let anything bad happen to him!" Laura said as she wrapped her arms around him.

"Let's slow down a little Laura," Mom instructed. "You haven't ridden him yet and don't know if he is the pony for you, or if we can afford him. Mrs. Taylor, how much are you asking for him?"

"I'm asking $950 for Rags and $450 for Pinocchio," Mrs. Taylor answered.

"That's more than I expected," Pop-Pop said, scratching his head. "I haven't bought a pony in a long time."

"I know it seems like a lot, but to be honest, I can't keep up with the demand. I haven't had two riding ponies for sale at the same time. The majority of them are sold as weanlings, around five months old," Mrs. Taylor explained. "Let's get going and Laura can ride both of them."

Laura and Rags headed towards the sand arena, with her dad closely behind. Mrs. Taylor headed into the barn to get Jodi.

"Dad, do you think we can buy Rags?" Laura asked.

"I don't know, it's more money than we planned to spend," Dad said, as he stroked Rags' neck.

"I can help!" Laura said. "I have twenty dollars we can put towards him."

"I appreciate that; let's have you ride him first!"

CHAPTER FOUR

"Does Rags remind you of somebody?" Mrs. Taylor asked Rose as she walked towards the ring.

"Yes," Rose said with a sad smile across her face.

"Trigger was an outstanding pony. I was so upset to hear what happened to him. My heart broke for you," Mrs. Taylor said. "I guess that's why you never rode again?"

"It was heartbreaking," Rose replied. "I couldn't find the strength to even go into the barn after that terrible day. It took me a long time to allow Laura to ride, but I can't protect her from everything."

"Sometimes the toughest lessons we learn in life are from what happens in the barn. I have lost many animals, but you just have to keep going and pray,"

Mrs. Taylor said. "I'm so proud of you for allowing your daughter to pursue her dreams, even though yours died with Trigger."

Rose nodded in agreement, trying to hold back the tears that welled up. She stopped at the gate and watched Mrs. Taylor head to the center of the arena, the place she loved the most. Jodi quickly joined Laura in the middle and proceeded to double-check her girth before mounting Pinocchio.

"Jodi, you take Rags and I'll have Laura ride Pinocchio first," Mrs. Taylor said, having the girls trade ponies.

"Gram, can I jump Rags a little?"

"No. Not after that stunt you pulled earlier," Mrs. Taylor firmly said. "Laura, go back to the barn and pick out a helmet that fits you and come right back."

Laura ran as fast as she could towards the barn and dusted the cobwebs from the first helmet she tried on. Then she darted back towards the ring. "No running around the ponies!" Mrs. Taylor said, stopping Laura in her tracks. Laura nervously resumed chewing her nails.

"It's okay. It's just that could spook them," Mrs. Taylor explained. "Now let me check that helmet to make sure it fits."

As Laura slowly walked towards Mrs. Taylor, she was startled by Jodi and Rags trotting right behind her.

"Jodi, you know better," Mrs. Taylor said strongly. "Laura, let's see how the helmet fits. It seems to fit good; how does it feel?"

"It feels perfect," Laura replied.

"Now let's check your stirrup length. Put the stirrup in your armpit and reach to the end of the leather, where it connects to the saddle."

Laura felt a bit clumsy and out of sorts as she stretched her fingertips towards the saddle. Pinocchio kept wiggling, making it difficult for Laura to accomplish her task. Mrs. Taylor checked the reins trying to encourage the pony to be still.

"They seem a little long. I'll shorten them about two holes," Mrs. Taylor said. She moved the buckles to the correct length. "Now, you should always check and adjust your girth before mounting. I already checked it, but you're the one riding. Can you put your fingers between the pony's side and the string girth?"

Laura took her fingers and easily put her whole hand between the girth and the pony's side. "It seems loose to me."

"That's correct. Good job. You passed the first test," she said with a smile. Something caught her attention. "Will you look at Jodi and Rags? She doesn't get to ride the nice ponies very often," Mrs. Taylor said, stopping to watch her granddaughter ride.

"How come she doesn't get to ride the nice ponies?" Laura asked.

"The nice ones sell quickly and don't stay around here for very long. Jodi helps break and train the young ones to get them ready to be sold."

"Does Jodi have her own pony?" Laura inquired.

"She did, but unfortunately, she died giving birth last year. Since then she's just been riding the young ones for me. We have a nice young mare coming along that I may give to her if she wants her, but she wouldn't be ready to ride at the fair this year," Mrs. Taylor said.

"How come you don't keep Rags for her to show at the fair?" Laura asked as she watched Jodi and Rags go around the ring in perfect harmony.

"I honestly never gave it a thought," Mrs. Taylor continued. "He has always been a sale pony when he's here. I have always given my grandchildren fillies, so they can have a dual purpose. One to be a riding pony for them and the other to produce babies. We better get going."

Jodi, smiling ear to ear, brought Rags to the walk, praising him for a job well done. Laura found herself uncontrollably jealous, wishing she could ride with such ease and perfection.

"Laura, give me your left leg, and when I count to

three, swing your right leg over the saddle," Mrs. Taylor instructed. "One, two, three, and up you go."

For the first time in her life, Laura found herself sitting on a pony. Pinocchio was not very patient, and he abruptly began to walk off before Laura was ready. Off she fell into the hot sand.

She quickly stood up and brushed the sand off, ready to try again. Her dad started to go to her. When he realized that she was fine, he returned to watch from the wooden benches.

Jodi, watching the fall, giggled uncontrollably.

"Are you okay?" Mrs. Taylor asked as she reprimanded the naughty pony.

"I'm fine. Can I try again?"

"Yes, but let's start with Rags first. I think Pinocchio may need some more training before you try him again. Oh, and congratulations! I always tell my students they need to fall off seven times to be a good rider! You're well on your way."

"I'll be a good rider soon then!" Laura said as she giggled, adjusting her helmet.

"Jodi, come over here. Can you get on him and let Laura ride Rags?" Mrs. Taylor asked.

"Sure, but she better be careful. Rags just spooked at the cow in the field next to the barn," Jodi said loudly.

"I think he will do just fine, young lady."

"Is Rags scared of cows?" Laura quickly asked.

"No, Jodi's scared that she won't be able to ride him anymore," Mrs. Taylor explained.

"I don't want to upset Jodi," Laura said. "If she wants to keep riding him, I can wait."

"She's fine, besides you're the one here for a lesson, and Jodi has ample opportunity to ride," Mrs. Taylor said.

Mrs. Taylor quickly gave Laura a leg up as Rags remained motionless. She explained how to hold the reins, and adjusted Laura's feet in the stirrups.

"Now, when you want him to move forward, give him a nudge or a light kick with your heels, but remember to always keep your heels down and your toes towards the sky. When you want to stop, sit up nice and tall, then pull gently on your reins to halt or stop him. To turn right, pull your right hand towards your knee, and the same for the left side. Got it?" Mrs. Taylor asked.

"Yes, ma'am," Laura answered. She had been preparing for this moment her entire life. "Are you sure he's okay with the cow?"

"Yes, I guarantee he won't care about the cow!" Mrs. Taylor assured her as she glared at Jodi attempting to control Pinocchio along the ring. "Well then, off you go."

"By myself?"

"Yes, make a figure eight and then come back to see me."

Laura gave Rags a nudge with her heels, and he obediently began to walk forward, waiting for the next cues. She successfully executed the figure eight and returned to the center of the ring for further instructions.

"Well done, Laura," Mrs. Taylor praised. "Now, let's start to work on trotting. I want you to walk to that end of the ring. When doing so, I want you to stand up for a second and then sit. That is how you post when trotting. On your way back to me, go ahead and squeeze a little harder and trot towards me doing the same thing."

Laura turned Rags and headed towards the end of the ring, feeling a bit anxious. They made the turn, and she squeezed her heels. He began to trot. At first, she bobbled back and forth until she found the rhythm. Posting was quite easy.

"Perfect job, Laura! You're a natural," Mrs. Taylor said with delight. "Now let's do that a couple more times and then your lesson will be over—"

"Gram, can I please jump Pinocchio?" Jodi said, interrupting Mrs. Taylor.

"No, not today. You need to head home soon, so you're not late for your pony club meeting," Mrs.

Taylor replied. "Did you see how well Laura did with Rags?"

"No, I wasn't watching. I'm finished with him. Could you turn him out for me?" Jodi asked.

"I can do that for you, but I hope the next time I see you that your attitude has improved. I would hate to have to tell your mother how bad it has been," Mrs. Taylor firmly said.

Jodi jumped off and nodded in agreement and quickly headed towards her house on the other side of the farm. Pinocchio watched her every move with bewilderment.

"Come over here, Laura, and let's have you dismount. Take both feet out of the stirrups and lean forward. Now, swing your right leg over and slide down. Did you enjoy your first lesson?"

"Yes, this has been the best day ever!" Laura said as she leaned in to hug Rags. Mrs. Taylor quickly turned and headed to the barn with Pinocchio in tow. Laura followed behind leading Rags.

"Let me help you," Pop-Pop said when he caught up to Laura in the barn. "Unbuckle the throat latch under his jaw, and now the noseband under his chin. Gently pull the top of the bridle over his ears and let the bit slowly out of his mouth. Well done, Laura."

"Pop-Pop, isn't he perfect? Can we buy him?" Laura asked.

"I think we need to talk to your parents. Let's brush him off and help Mrs. Taylor turn him out first."

Laura carefully removed the saddle and saddle pad off of Rags. Then she thoroughly brushed him and led him to his field. Mrs. Taylor followed her with Pinocchio and turned both boys out at the same time. The two ponies found a suitable spot in the field and enjoyed a much-deserved roll in the mud.

Rose, John, and Mom-Mom were watching the mares and foals play together in a field dotted with buttercups when Laura ran up from behind.

"Mom, can we buy Rags? He is really sweet! I love him so much!"

"He sure is nice and we would love to be able to get him, but he's almost double what we thought a pony would cost," Mom said as she started to fix Laura's ponytail.

"Laura, we're going to go home to talk about it. Your grandparents said they could help too, but we still need to think about it," Dad said.

"I understand. Thank you so much for today. I have never been so happy!" Laura said as Mrs. Taylor approached the family.

"Good job today, young lady," Mrs. Taylor said. "I overheard you say that you're going to think about buying Rags. I think he would be very suitable, but I understand about the financial end of it too. If you could let me know by tomorrow, that would be great. I have another family interested in him too, but I will wait to call them back until I hear from you."

"Thank you," Pop-Pop replied. "We really appreciate the understanding. I guess I should have asked you the cost before coming, and we could have been more prepared. I'll call you tomorrow afternoon. Again, thanks so much."

The family headed towards their vehicles after saying goodbye to Mrs. Taylor. "This has been one of the best days ever," John said, as he ran up, grabbed Laura, and threw her over his shoulder.

"John, we may have to get you a pony too!" Mom-Mom said as she opened the car door. "We'll meet you at the house for dinner, and then we can talk after dinner about Rags."

"Awesome! I'm so excited you are coming for dinner too!" Laura said loudly. "We have a lot to figure out, and we can count my money too!"

CHAPTER FIVE

Sunday evening was full of discussion and yummy food. The family cleaned up dinner and began to discuss the purchase of Rags. Laura scurried to her room to grab her beloved piggy bank to contribute to the transaction.

"Rose and I have $500.00 we've set aside for a pony, but I'm sure we could come up with a little bit more," John said, as they sat at the kitchen table. Laura returned from her room.

"If Mrs. Taylor won't take less and we need to pay full price, do you think she would throw in a saddle and bridle?" Rose asked while drying her hands with a tattered dish towel.

"We can ask, but in my experience with her, she is

a savvy businesswoman and won't negotiate," Pop-Pop replied. "I would think we would need $75 for a saddle and bridle, so that would be a total of $1,025 for everything. We've been saving for a pony as well, since Laura was born, hoping one day we would need it. We have $400 to add. How much do you have Laura?"

"I think it's around $20, but let's break it open and find out."

Laura's dad gently took the piggy bank to the counter, wrapped it in a towel, and grabbed a crab mallet. He hit the towel with the mallet, breaking the blue bank into multiple pieces. Dollar bills, change, and some lint were exposed. He carefully picked through broken glass. Laura waited impatiently beside her father. He placed the money in the middle of the table to begin the counting process. All four adults and Laura grabbed a handful and started tallying the funds.

"Alright, I think you have $42.75," Mom said, after adding up all the totals. "So, the total all together with our money and your grandparents is $942.75 leaving us short $82.25."

"Don't worry about that," Mom-Mom said. "I have been wanting to declutter and sell some excess stuff anyway. I can sell my silver bowl and I know I can get $75 for it."

"Your mother gave you that bowl. Are you sure you want to sell it?" Pop-Pop asked. Laura sat on the edge of her seat in anticipation.

"I think she would understand. She wouldn't want her great-granddaughter to have a pony and no tack to ride him. I can take it to the antique store tomorrow."

"Mom, we may be able to come up with the difference," Rose said, with her hands folded.

"I'm not changing my mind," Mom-Mom replied. "We are going to need money for hay, feed, and vet bills, so save your money for those expenses. Looks like we are adding a pony to the family!"

"Yeah!" Laura said happily. She quickly stood up and hugged each one of the adults at the table. "I can't wait. I can't believe it! This is going to be the best summer of my life!"

"I hope you can get through the last week of school," Mom said. "Dad, can you call Mrs. Taylor in the morning and let her know we can buy Rags?"

"No problem," Pop-Pop said. "I'll ask her if she can deliver him next Saturday. That will give me this week to get the barn ready."

"Perfect, but we can help too," John said. "I can pick Laura up from school tomorrow and we can start cleaning the barn."

"Sounds like we have a plan," Mom-Mom said as

she stood up to prepare to head home. "Laura, you better get to bed, you have a big week ahead of you."

Laura's grandparents headed home, and she got ready for bed. Her parents kissed her goodnight. Laura laid in bed trying to fall asleep. Her mind was racing in the pure excitement of owning Rags. She quietly snuck out of bed and rearranged her dresser. She was able to make the perfect spot to display the state fair trophy.

F inally, the bell rang, and school was finished for the day. Laura bolted out the door to meet her mother in the parking lot. Much to her surprise, it wasn't her mother waiting for her, but her wise ol' grandfather.

"Pop-Pop, what are you doing here?" Laura asked, jumping into his truck.

"I called your mom and asked if I could pick you up today, so we could go pay Mrs. Taylor for Rags," he said, driving out the school lane. "We have all the money together, and I told her we would stop by today and pay for him. Mrs. Taylor is going to deliver him Saturday afternoon, so since you have half a day of school on Friday, we will clean the barn then and you can spend the night."

"Yeah!" Laura said, smiling ear to ear. "I can't believe it! God answered all my prayers."

The drive to Hadley Farm was full of chatter from Laura. Her enthusiasm was overflowing. When they pulled in the driveway, Laura hopped out to walk down the bumpety ol' lane and take in the wonderful beauty and tranquility.

Mrs. Taylor had just come up from the barn and stood on her rustic-covered porch when Pop-Pop arrived.

"Are you here for your lesson?" Mrs. Taylor asked coyly.

"Not today. I forgot my crop," he said happily. "Laura is walking down the lane. She can't get enough time around your ponies. I have the money for Rags with me."

"That's great. Are you in a hurry?" Mrs. Taylor asked as she headed to the front door.

"No, I think Laura could stay here forever," he replied.

"I have to call the vet," Mrs. Taylor said, slipping her shoes off. "I'll be twenty minutes and I'll meet you down at the barn."

Pop-Pop nodded his head in agreement and proceeded to go find Laura. He headed towards the orchard pasture where the mares and foals resided. The young foals stayed close to their mothers but would venture away from them, only to quickly return to the safety of Mom. Laura startled Pop-Pop after popping out from behind a gigantic oak tree.

"You about gave me a heart attack, young lady," Pop-Pop jokingly said.

"Is he ours?" Laura anxiously asked.

"Not yet," Pop-Pop answered, mesmerized by the babies frolicking in the field. "I'm going to meet her down at the barn after she makes a phone call to the vet."

"Can I go see Rags while we wait?"

"You sure can," he replied. "I'll meet you down there in a few. I'm going to hang out here for a while and watch the foals."

Laura ran quickly towards the red barn. She saw her adored pony heading into the stable with Jodi. Mrs. Taylor was close behind the duo. Laura stopped to catch her breath. She didn't want to be huffing and puffing when she entered the barn. The closer she got, she could hear Jodi arguing with her grandmother. Laura decided to wait until the heated exchange quieted down. She stood on the side of the arn entrance waiting.

"Who am I going to ride at the fair this year if you sell him?" Jodi said frustrated.

"Jodi, please do not raise your voice at me," Mrs. Taylor scolded as she stood in the tack room door. "I've already committed to selling him and I cannot go back on my word. Pinocchio should be ready."

"Pinocchio!" Jodi shouted standing in the aisle. "He's so green and he's never been to a show. Why am I the one who always has to train all the ponies, but never gets to ride the nice ones? I would love to win the trophy just once."

"Jodi, that's what your sisters always did for me when they were your age," Mrs. Taylor quietly explained. "This is my business. I breed and sell my ponies, and I appreciate all your help. I'm so sorry that Helen died having her foal last year. I know it broke your heart, and I will find you another pony, it just may not be in time for the fair this year."

"I only have two more years to ride at the fair," Jodi said as tears strolled down her face. "Both my sisters won the fair trophy many times, and I haven't even once had the chance. I really miss Helen and Rags reminds me so much of her, it makes riding fun again."

Laura listened in disbelief, realizing her dream coming true would cause Jodi's to not. She leaned up against the barn, resting her head on the chipping red paint. The happiest day of her life had now become the most challenging.

Mrs. Taylor walked over to her distraught grand-daughter, embracing her as she cried. "I had no idea how you loved him; if I would have known I wouldn't have sold him. But I can't and won't go back on my word. I love you and I'm very sorry."

Laura thought to herself, *If we buy Rags today, Jodi is going to be crushed and hate me forever. I was so jealous of her; she lives on this beautiful farm with all of these ponies and gets to ride all the time. I just didn't have any idea that she didn't have her own pony. I have to go tell Pop-Pop we can't buy him.*

Laura met her grandfather midway on his way to the barn, trying to hold back her tears.

"What's wrong, Laura?" Pop-Pop asked with concern.

"We can't buy Rags," Laura said as tears rolled down her dusty cheeks. "Not today, not ever!"

"I don't understand, what happened?"

"I don't want him anymore or ever. Can we please leave?" Laura pleaded.

Mrs. Taylor made her way out of the barn and heard the confusion between Laura and her grandfather. "Laura, did you hear Jodi and me arguing?"

"I did, but I didn't mean to," Laura replied, pulling her shirt up to wipe her eyes.

"What's going on?" Pop-Pop asked, feeling confused.

"I'm so sorry, Laura," Mrs. Taylor confessed. "I didn't realize how much Rags meant to Jodi and she was pretty upset to hear that I sold him. I will find her another pony. I don't want you to feel bad about this. I told your grandfather I would sell him to you and I will not go back on my word."

"I don't want him anymore," Laura said, holding back tears. "Please let Jodi keep him and ride him at the fair. Can I go wait for you in the truck, Pop-Pop?"

"Of course, but are you sure?" Pop-Pop said, putting his arm around her.

Laura nodded in agreement as she headed towards the truck. The joy she had earlier was depleted and gone.

"I'm so sorry for all of this," Mrs. Taylor said in despair. "I feel terrible. Let me have Jodi work with Pinocchio and see if he comes around. I have to do something."

"Let me know how he comes along," Pop-Pop said as he reached out to shake her hand. "Laura will be okay; she's one tough cookie."

"I'll be in touch soon. You should be very proud of your beautiful granddaughter and how mature she is."

Pop-Pop and Laura drove home in silence. Laura stared out the window and was unable to find a daydream to take her mind off of losing her dream pony. Pop-Pop was just as distraught as his grand-daughter and his mind raced trying to fix the dilemma.

"I'm so proud of you today," Pop-Pop said as he patted her leg. "I know how hard that was for you."

Laura slowly nodded and acknowledged him.

"Why don't we go to an auction this weekend?" Pop-Pop asked. "Maybe we can find a saddle and you can see all the horses and ponies. Would you like that?"

"Yes, I would love that," Laura replied, perking up a little. "I can't wait!"

CHAPTER SIX

L aura woke up very early Saturday at her grandparents' house. She ran downstairs to find Pop-Pop drinking coffee out of his favorite green cup.

"Good morning, Laura," Pop-Pop said. Laura climbed into his lap and hugged him. She laid her head on his strong shoulders.

"What time are we leaving?" she asked.

"Let's say around 10:00 a.m. That will give us time to stop and eat lunch on the way."

Just then, Mom-Mom called them into the kitchen for breakfast. Laura hardly touched the pancakes and sausages Mom-Mom had piled high on her plate. After taking a few bites, she rushed upstairs to get dressed. She was so excited about the sale. She sat on the edge of the bed pulling her socks up. *I hope we find a pony today!* she thought.

She heard Pop-Pop turn the ignition of the old Chevrolet truck and knew it was time to go.

Laura ran out the front door when she heard Mom-Mom ask her, "Don't I get a kiss goodbye?"

"Oops, sorry!" She stopped in her tracks and gave Mom-Mom a kiss and a hug.

"Sweetie," Mom-Mom said. "Remember, no buying a pony today! We want a Hadley pony, and maybe Pinocchio will be ready before you know it."

With a big sigh, Laura responded quickly, "I know Mom-Mom, but it will be fun to look!"

"Laura, I told Pop-Pop the same thing. The two of you going to the auction together makes me nervous," Mom-Mom said with a smirk.

Laura and Pop-Pop headed down the driveway. It was such a beautiful drive. The trees were at their peak of fullness. As they got closer to the sale, Amish buggies pulled by sturdy horses lined the side of the road. Laura looked at each horse with curiosity, wondering if they enjoyed their job.

"How are you doing with the whole Rags situation?" Pop-Pop asked.

"Okay, I guess," Laura answered, picking at the seam of her jeans. "I was so happy that my mom and dad understood."

"Your mother handled it better than I thought she would."

"I sure hope Jodi is happy now. I want to watch her ride at the fair this year."

"Maybe you'll be competing there yourself," Pop-Pop said with encouragement. Laura shrugged her shoulders in disbelief as they traveled on.

Pop-Pop slowly pulled into the diner parking lot where they were going to eat lunch. It was an old diner that he'd visited for years. The Willow Diner was small, sparsely decorated with a few horse pictures, and never seemed to change at all. But the home-cooked food was tasty and reasonably priced. They sat in a cozy booth facing each other and ordered lunch.

"The food at the auction isn't very good, so eat up here," Pop-Pop said.

"Okay," Laura said. "How many horses do you think will be there?"

"Probably quite a few. Camps are looking for horses and ponies this time of year. Prices might be higher than in the fall. It can be expensive to feed them hay all winter long. The dealers hope to make the money back at the auctions in the spring," Pop-Pop said.

"Who buys the horses?" Laura asked with interest.

"It's hard to know who the buyers are. Some are looking for horses for themselves to trail ride or to show. Sometimes horse trainers buy them to get a bargain. They take them home and retrain them, hoping to make a profit by selling them for more money. Then there are the dealers who will buy anything hoping to resell and make money," Pop-Pop continued. "They usually own feedlots and small paddocks, where horses are kept in large groups. It's a cheap way to care for them. The dealers keep the horses there and try to sell them to individuals or take them to a different auction, or take them home and fatten them up. Those horses are treated like inventory in a store, not like a living animal," Pop-Pop said. "We better get going."

There was no response from Laura as they left the diner and made their way back into the truck. She stared out the window of the vehicle and thought assuredly to herself, *One day, when I have my own pony, I'm going to keep it forever.*

Laura and Pop-Pop pulled into the auction about an hour before it started, just as the rain was letting up. There were horse trailers of all different kinds. Some were as big as tractor-trailers, others were just long enough for one horse. A few people were bringing horses into the auction barn. There was a small riding ring where the horses could be tried by anyone.

Laura and Pop-Pop parked the truck and headed to watch the action in the ring. The temperature had dropped after the brief rain shower, and it had become a bit chilly. This didn't help the horses' behavior. The fresh, cool air had just started blowing across the ring, and like a chain reaction, the horses threw their heads back, snorted, and in two instances, bucked their riders off! Laura and Pop-Pop leaned on the fence that enclosed the ring and tried to get a good view.

Chaos reigned. The two loose horses, feeling very fresh, bolted around as the other riders tried to control their mounts. Eventually, everyone decided to dismount and wait for someone to catch the mischievous horses. Soon, everything settled down. Laura was mesmerized by all the activity and took it all in. She could have stayed there all day.

"We better get inside before we get too cold," Pop-Pop said. Laura didn't respond. She just turned and followed him into the sale barn. Pop-Pop knew his way around the barn. He led Laura through the aisle way where potential buyers and dealers examined horses.

Pop-Pop stopped at the end of the aisle and started to talk with an old friend. As they talked, Laura watched the activity. The barn was old, with cobwebs lining the ceiling. The smell of musky hay covered the floor with manure scattered all around. So many different noises filled the air. Horses, whinnying for friends they had been separated from, could be loud at times. A lot of chatter was going on between the dealers and potential buyers.

"This fine Quarter Horse gelding was shown all year by a ten-year-old boy. He won multiple year-end championships," one big-bellied dealer told a couple examining his horse.

The couple asked, "Why did they sell him?"

The portly dealer quickly explained, "After winter, the kid lost interest, so they called me, and I went and picked him up. You won't find a nicer horse anywhere."

Doubting the truthfulness of the story, the couple walked away. When a lady inquired about another of his horses, the plump seller used the same sales pitch. Listening to the dealer's similar tales, Laura thought to herself, *Why are they here if the horses are so amazing?*

She realized that the dealers told the same story about different horses to anyone who showed interest. Laura started to tug on Pop-Pop's jacket, trying to get his attention.

"Are you okay, Laura?" Pop-Pop asked when he saw Laura dancing from one foot to the other.

"I really need to go to the bathroom."

Pop-Pop said goodbye to his friend, and they walked in the direction of the bathrooms. There were so many horses and ponies in the aisle way that they would walk ten steps and have to stop for a while. Not wanting to be separated from his granddaughter, Pop-Pop held Laura's hand firmly. His warm, tight grip made her feel secure.

"I'm doing my best to get you to the potty; are you okay?" Pop-Pop asked.

"Yeah, I'm okay."

They finally made the turn into the side aisle where the bathrooms were.

The aisle was where the auction kept the ponies and young horses. The washroom was in sight when Pop-Pop suddenly stopped in his tracks. He was staring at a small Shetland-type pony. She was covered in dry mud, with burrs in her mane and tail. He could barely see her face, but he saw her magnificent dark eyes filled with despair.

Pop-Pop found a way to get Laura to her destination and ordered, "Hurry up. There's a pony I want us to take a look at."

"What kind of pony?" Laura asked.

"Just go to the bathroom and then I'll show you."

Laura hurried into the ladies' room while Pop-Pop stood guard at the door.

CHAPTER SEVEN

L aura came running out of the washroom, hitting
Pop-Pop with the door by accident. "I'm sorry.
Are you okay?"

"I'm fine," Pop-Pop said as he chuckled. "Let's go
look at that pony."

Pop-Pop carefully made his way past the bigger
ponies while making sure to keep Laura safe. They
went to the aisle where the pony stood, head hung low,
looking dejected. She appeared to be in rough shape
and very displeased at being tied beside larger ponies.

He put his hand out, allowing the pitiful pony to
smell him. Her velvet muzzle felt warm in his palm. He
pushed her excessive forelock to the side, trying to see
what was underneath. He saw the most beautiful
dished face, with wide, somber eyes, and petite ears.

"Laura! Take a look at her," Pop-Pop said. Laura slowly walked up to the pony. The pony softly nickered to her in a quiet voice.

With an enormous smile, Laura said, "You are sweet. What are you doing here?" Laura gave her a pat on the neck. She was surprised to feel so much cold and hard mud caked on the miserable mare.

"She's a mess," Pop-Pop said. "This poor thing has been neglected for some time."

Laura found a brush buried in the musty straw next to the hayrack and began to groom her. As Laura moved the brush in a clockwise circle, the pony curled her lip in delight, closing her eyes, enjoying the moment.

"She likes that," Pop-Pop noticed. "I'm sure it's been a long time since she's had any attention. As Laura moved the mud away from the pony's coat, she could feel small, crust-like bumps under her hair.

"Pop-Pop, what's this all over her back?" Laura asked. Pop-Pop took a look at what Laura had found.

"It's rain rot," he said. "That's what happens when a pony isn't brushed regularly. Watch what happens when I pick it off. See the bloody spot? It can be painful to remove, and she has a severe case of it."

Just then, a grouchy-looking old man headed their way, seeing them with the pony.

"Can I help you?" he asked.

"Just taking a look at this pony," Pop-Pop said. "How old is she?"

"I don't know. Got her papers somewhere. She ain't much to look at," the surly man replied.

"Where did you get her?" Pop-Pop asked.

"A lady called me after her great aunt died and needed to get rid of her. I picked her up this morning and brought her here. I think the lady was scared of her. She's probably afraid of her own shadow!" the man said.

"I am Jack Anderson, and this is my granddaughter Laura," Pop-Pop said as he extended his right hand. "What's your name?"

"Don," he answered curtly.

"You said she has papers. Can I take a look at them?" Pop-Pop asked.

"I think they're at the sale's office," Don said. "The lady just paid me to haul her here. Doesn't matter much to me what this pony brings. It'll cost the lady more to haul her here than what she's gonna get for her. I've got a really nice lesson pony over here if you want to look at him."

"No thanks. We're just interested in this one," Pop-Pop said.

"I think you're wasting your time," Don said, as he walked away.

Laura and Pop-Pop looked at each other with confusion.

"He's not very nice!" Laura said with a frown.

"No, he's not. It's a shame we couldn't see the pony's papers before the sale starts," Pop-Pop remarked.

Just then, an announcement came over the loudspeaker, "The sale will start in ten minutes. We have eighty-seven head of horses to see today."

Pop-Pop took a long look at the pony and noticed she was Hip Number Five. Every horse has a sticker on the hindquarters to identify it. Each horse takes about one minute to sell.

"Come on, sweetie," Pop-Pop said, "Let's go find a spot to sit. She's covered in rain rot and that can be a nightmare to deal with."

Gently petting the animal's face, Laura was reluctant to leave the pony's side.

"What do you think of her? Do you like her? She's really gentle. I think she would be a perfect pony for me."

"She looks kind, but we don't know anything about her. Remember what Mom-Mom said? We don't want to get a pony that isn't safe," Pop-Pop said. "Let's go sit down. She looks well-bred, but we just don't have time to learn more about her."

"But Pop-Pop, she shouldn't be here. I *know* she's a good pony, and she needs us!" Laura pleaded.

"Come on," Pop-Pop said firmly. "I'm sorry. We can't buy a pony we know nothing about!"

Laura gave the pony a hug and a kiss and whispered, "Goodbye." She could feel a lump in her throat as she walked away with Pop-Pop. They found seats at the top of the grandstand. The seats were made of wood, and they were not very comfortable.

There was a twenty-foot lane between rows of gates where the horses trotted back and forth, where the bidding took place. Various dealers leaned on the gates to have a closer look at the horses being sold. The auctioneer read a list of rules and terms before the official bidding started. Pop-Pop leaned over and said to Laura, "Don't point at anything or raise your hand. The auctioneer will think you're bidding."

"I won't," Laura promised. Pop-Pop could see the disappointment on her face and felt responsible for getting her excited about the pony.

Hip Number One came into the sale's ring. The bidding began, with the first horse selling for $225. The auctioneer started in on the second horse, which sold for $550.

"That was a nice horse, wasn't it, Laura?" Pop-Pop asked.

Laura pretended to be interested. "Yeah. He was

fancy. I don't really understand the man selling them, or for how much. He talks too fast."

"That's what an auctioneer does. He tries to get you caught up in the moment, not giving you time to think. Just listen to the price he says before he drops the hammer to finalize the sale."

"I think I understand now."

As the third horse sold, Laura could see the dear pony she had brushed and with whom she had briefly fallen in love. The pony looked so scared and worried, which caused Laura concern. She wondered where the mare would be going.

The fourth horse left the ring after having been sold for $75. The auctioneer began to describe Number Five.

"Hip Number Five is a registered Shetland Pony. She is eight years old. Her owner recently passed away."

The bidding started at $100, but since there was no audience interest, it quickly dropped to $50, and then to $25. The big-bellied dealer raised his hand and then another dealer nodded his head. The bid was now at $55. Laura looked at Pop-Pop and gave him a nudge.

Pop-Pop was struggling with what to do. He wanted that pony as much as Laura did. Without hesitation, he raised his hand and said, "Hold on, can you tell me her registered name?"

Annoyed by the interruption, the auctioneer stopped and looked at Hip Number Five's papers. "Uh, looks like, 'Hadley Spider,' he responded, and proceeded with the sale.

Hearing the Hadley name, Pop-Pop and Laura looked at each other in pure shock. "Pop-Pop, we *have* to get her!" Laura quietly pleaded.

Without delay, Pop-Pop raised his hand and joined in the bidding.

The portly dealer also knew of the Hadley Pony Farm and knew that the pony was worth more than originally anticipated.

The auctioneer was at $82 when the stout dealer raised his hand agreeing to the current price.

"How about $90 for this little darling?" the auctioneer asked Pop-Pop. Pop-Pop nodded his head accepting the price. As the next bid went to the other bidder.

The bidding went back to Pop-Pop at the price of $100. Pop-Pop had to think about it for a minute.

Laura saw the concern in her grandfather's anxious face, and asked, "What's wrong, Pop-Pop?"

"I only have $100 with me. Just worried I won't have enough money," Pop-Pop answered.

Laura's facial expression went from exuberance to total misery. Feeling helpless, Pop-Pop looked over at Laura and agreed to the current bid. He knew that this would be the last bid he could place, and he waited to see if his opponent would out-bid him. Pop-Pop wrapped his arm around Laura as they waited.

The big-bellied dealer took a moment to think about the price. When he looked up to see who the remaining bidder was, he saw a little girl filled with distress. He paused and shook his head no, and passed the bid on.

Hip Number Five. The warm-hearted dealer glanced up at Laura, who beamed with his decision. He winked and smiled at her. The joy he felt at that moment was worth more than money to him.

The auctioneer looked around to check for other bidders. Seeing no one else, he pointed toward Pop-Pop and dropped the hammer!

CHAPTER EIGHT

"I can't believe we got her," Laura quietly said to Pop-Pop.

"She's ours. We better go pay for her," Pop-Pop said. "And then, we need to figure out how we are going to get her home." Laura and her grandfather carefully made their way down the grandstand while the auction continued. When they saw the big-bellied dealer, Pop-Pop stopped and shook his hand.

"I want to say thanks," Pop-Pop said. "My name is Jack Anderson, and this is my granddaughter, Laura."

"You don't need to thank me. I'm Smoke Edwards, but everyone calls me 'Smokey,'" the dealer said. "That could be a nice pony you bought."

"Hopefully she is, under all that thick hair and crusty mud," Pop-Pop replied. "Guess we'll have to

wait until she sheds her coat to see what we have."
Trying to hide the real reason he stopped bidding,
Smokey explained that the pony might have been too
much of a risk for him.

"We better go to the sale's office and settle up the
pony. Have a good night," Pop-Pop said to Smokey.

"Thanks, and good luck with that mare," Smokey
said. The men shook hands, and Pop-Pop headed
toward the office.

"Come on, Laura," he said.

Laura looked up at Smokey and grinned with
appreciation. Smokey gave her a tender pat on the
head. Laura hurried along to catch up with her
grandfather.

In front of them, horses bustled in and out of the
sale's ring and the crowd thickened. Dealers and
buyers wove their way around long lines of hungry
people queued up in front of food stalls. It would be a
challenge just to reach the stairs leading up to the
office, and those stairs seemed endless to Laura.

Pop-Pop reached the cashier, a bit out of breath
and feeling overwhelmed as the reality of buying Hip
Number Five began to sink in.

The cashier handed Pop-Pop an invoice for the
pony. "That will be $100 even. Here are her registra-
tion papers," she said.

Pop-Pop pulled out his wallet from his back pocket, took out all of the cash, and handed it to her.

After counting the money carefully, the cashier marked, "Paid in Full" on the invoice.

"Thank you," she said. "And remember, all animals must be removed from the premises by 9:00 p.m. tonight. If you need to make arrangements for hauling, you can go to the stabling office."

"No problem," Pop-Pop said, knowing full well that he didn't have a plan for getting the pony home.

Laura and Pop-Pop left the office and headed toward where the pony stood waiting for them.

Laura could see her all alone. The pony appeared to be filled with worry. But when she saw Laura, she picked her head up, pricked her ears, and softly nickered.

"It's okay, girl. Nothing bad is going to happen to you now. I will always take care of you," Laura whispered in her ear. "What are we going to call her?" Laura asked her grandfather.

"Well, her registered name is 'Hadley Spider.' Would you like to call her 'Spider?'" Pop-Pop asked.

Shivers ran down Laura's back. She shook her head. "No! I'm scared of spiders!"

Pop-Pop chuckled, "Well then, do you have any other ideas?"

Without hesitation, Laura said, "Let's call her 'Sugar,' because she's so sweet!"

"That's perfect," Pop-Pop agreed. Then, in a more serious tone, he added, "We better find her a way home."

Pop-Pop knew that most horse shippers required to be paid upfront. He hoped to find someone to haul her home who would accept payment when dropping Sugar at her new home. "Laura, stay here with Sugar. I'll be right back," he said.

"Wh-Where are you going?" Laura asked nervously.

"I need to arrange transportation for Sugar. I'm just going to the stable office," he said, pointing, "at the end of this aisle. If you need me, I'll be close by," Pop-Pop assured her.

Laura stood very close to Sugar, delicately stroking her cheek, when someone tapped her on the shoulder, making her jump. It was Smokey!

"Didn't mean to startle you," he said. "Where's your Grandpa?"

"He went to the stable office to find someone to help us take Sugar home," Laura answered anxiously.

"How far away is she going?"

"It's about an hour and a half away, I think," Laura said. "Close to Baltimore."

"No problem," Smokey said. "I can take her; let's go find your Grandpa and let him know."

Smokey and Laura headed toward the stable office when Pop-Pop came out. The reality of buying a pony and having to have to tell Mom-Mom was almost unbearable. He was unable to arrange transportation. Lost in his thoughts, he didn't even see Smokey and Laura walking straight at him.

"Jack!" Smokey yelled. "I was looking for you. I'm getting ready to leave and can ship the pony for you."

With much surprise and relief, Pop-Pop answered, "That would be great! I'm short on cash now, but when we get there—"

Smokey interrupted him, "We'll worry about that later; let's get the pony loaded. I drive a blue and tan Ford dually, with a beige six-horse gooseneck trailer. It's parked in the first row of rigs. I'll meet you there in twenty minutes."

"Did you buy any horses today?" Pop-Pop questioned.

"Nope, didn't see anything I liked, and I sold the two I brought with me. The pony will have the trailer all to herself. Hopefully, she won't get lost in there. I need to go to the sales office," Smokey said as he chuckled.

"Sugar will feel like royalty," Pop-Pop said. "Could Laura stay with you? I need to run to the restroom."

"Come on, Laura," Smokey said as he and Laura headed towards the office.

"Hey doll," Smokey said to the receptionist. "I came to get a check for Hip Numbers Seven and Twelve," Smokey said, flirting with the office staff.

"Are you kidding?" the cashier asked. "The auction isn't half over and you've never left without buying something."

"I'm helping out my new friend Laura," he said, nodding in her direction.

"That's awful nice of you, Smokey," she said, handing him his check. "Have a good night; I'll see you next week!"

"We'll see," Smokey replied. "Take care of yourself." A few, cold-hearted dealers in the past have had a special moment in their lives like Smokey had just experienced, which enabled them to feel true compassion. Once that happened, they might not stay in the business of dealing horses.

Pop-Pop, Laura, and Smokey headed to the parking lot with Sugar. "I'll lead her to the trailer, Laura. I want to make sure she isn't silly," Pop-Pop explained. After leading her for a bit without any commotion, he said, "Here, Laura, you can take her now." He handed her the rope. "She's not skittish at all." Laura took the lead line in her right hand, gathering the extra line in her left hand. She was very careful not to wrap the rope around her hand. Smokey stopped briefly to chat with an old friend.

"Good job, Laura," Pop-Pop smiled. "That's perfect, the way you're leading her."

"Mrs. Taylor taught me how to lead a pony when we worked with Rags," Laura told him.

Smokey caught up to them. He saw Laura leading Sugar.

"Hey, Jack," he hollered. "Do you see my rig?"

"Yes," Pop- Pop said as he waited for him, while Laura kept walking ahead with Sugar.

As the two men watched Laura leading Sugar, Pop-Pop put his hand on Smokey's shoulder and said, "Wish I had a camera!"

"You don't need one," Smokey said. "You'll have that snapshot in your head forever." After Sugar was loaded into the trailer, they headed home. Smokey followed their Chevy truck. Laura couldn't take her eyes off the trailer.

"You're going to get a stiff neck," Pop-Pop said with a warning.

"Oh, Pop-Pop, I'll be fine. I can't wait to get her home!" Laura proclaimed.

"I sure hope we're not in too much trouble with your grandmother," Pop-Pop shared.

Just then, the reality of having to tell Mom-Mom and her parents hit Laura too. She turned forward and stopped watching the trailer. Laura stared at the road ahead, feeling like she'd just swallowed a brick. It felt like it was sitting at the bottom of her stomach.

"Pop-Pop, do you think we're going to be in big trouble?" Laura asked apprehensively.

"I don't know, Laura, but I'm pretty sure we won't be allowed to go anywhere without Mom-Mom or your parents with us from now on," Pop-Pop answered, trying to make light of the situation.

Seeing how worried Laura was, he added quickly, "It'll be okay; they'll love Sugar."

"Yeah, how could you *not* fall in love with her?" Laura asked.

As they made the turn into Pop-Pop's driveway, they could see the lights in the house and Laura's parents' car. They glanced at each other at the same time and were speechless.

CHAPTER NINE

J ohn, Rose, and Mom-Mom relaxed at the kitchen table just after dinner.

"Mom," Rose said, "dinner was delicious."

"Thanks, dear. Would you like some coffee? It could be a long time waiting on Laura and your dad."

Then John noticed something out of the kitchen window. He exclaimed, "Hey, I see headlights! I think they're home!"

"Laura is going to be tired tonight. It's been a long day," Rose said.

"I don't believe it!" Mom-Mom continued, changing her tone. "There's a truck and trailer following them!"

Mom-Mom and Rose stared out the window in disbelief.

"Come on, let's go see what's in the trailer!" John said, smiling. He grabbed his jacket and hurried out.

Shaking her head, Mom-Mom looked at her daughter, "John is as bad as your father!"

Rose sighed and nodded, "John reminds me a *lot* of Daddy."

Rose could see the distress on her mother's face. She remembered as a little girl when Pop-Pop would return from auctions and sales with all kinds of destitute horses. Mom-Mom would be irritated, at first, but after seeing the pitiful animals, she always opened her heart up to them.

Deep in thought, Mom-Mom sat on the worn-out mahogany stool by the kitchen door, staring at the sink stacked with soiled dishes.

Rose prodded her. "Come on, Mom. Let's go see what they brought home." Rose and Mom-Mom put on their coats. Rose took Mom-Mom's hand and kissed her on the cheek as they headed toward the barn.

"Laura, wait in the truck," Pop-Pop ordered. He parked on the grass next to the lane, hoping to make room for Smokey's huge rig. Smokey pulled up next to Pop-Pop's truck and turned off the clanging diesel engine.

Pop-Pop went into the barn, trying to find the lights. It took a while for him to make his way through the maze of cobwebs that lined the deserted stable. Pop-Pop wiped his face and flipped the switch. The lights slowly blinked on and off until they warmed up. The barn appeared to be completely coated with filthy cobwebs.

Smokey walked into the aisle and bellowed, "What a mess! Guess nothing has been living in here for a while."

Smokey chuckled as he found a broom and began clearing a path into the first stall on the right.

"It's been about five years since I've been in here," Pop-Pop said. "After we sold the last horse, it made me heartsick to see the barn empty."

"I can only imagine," Smokey said as he willingly tended to the unlivable stall.

Sugar became restless in the trailer all by herself and whinnied, hoping to hear a familiar voice. When there was no response, she became silent.

"Go help Laura with the pony, and I'll finish the stall," Smokey said.

Pop-Pop nodded and moved quickly toward his truck. As he approached it, he noticed John was just reaching the barn.

John had a big smile on his face. "What did you bring home?"

"John, you wouldn't believe it if I told you," Pop-Pop answered. "Here—look at the papers." Pop-Pop pulled the documents out of his shirt pocket and handed them to John.

"Dad, she's a Hadley pony from Mrs. Taylor's farm!" Laura blurted out before her father could open the envelope. John was surprised to hear the Hadley Farm name. Mom-Mom and Rose were close enough to hear Laura.

"Did you say it's a Hadley pony?" Mom-Mom questioned.

As soon as Laura heard Mom-Mom, she turned and ran over to her grandmother and her mom. She wrapped her arms around Mom-Mom, nestling her head into Mom-Mom's cozy coat.

"She's a real Hadley pony, Mom-Mom! Her name is Sugar!" Laura announced. "Come on," Laura gestured to her mother and grandmother. "Let's go see her!"

Laura took Mom-Mom's hand and grabbed Rose's jacket. Sugar's excited new owner directed the two of them to the back of the horse trailer.

Pop-Pop and John followed behind the ladies. Hearing the discussion, Sugar began to chatter again. Pop-Pop opened the large back door of the enormous trailer. Staring back at them was a very needy pony.

"It's okay, girl; you're home now," Laura coaxed her. "Isn't she the most beautiful pony ever?"

"Oh my goodness," Mom-Mom said, catching her

breath. "That sorrowful, dear, old pony needs some tender loving care!"

With much relief, Pop-Pop put his arm around Mom-Mom. "I knew you would understand why we couldn't leave her at the auction."

"We better get her into the barn; she's had a long day," Rose suggested.

Sugar was relieved to be out of the trailer. She looked around at her new home and sighed loudly. Then, she lowered her head and began to eat the lush grass at her feet.

"She seems right at home," Smokey declared, stepping out of the barn.

"I would agree with that," Pop-Pop nodded. He introduced Smokey to the family.

"Thanks for bringing Sugar home. You've made our little girl very happy," John reached into his back pocket, pulling out his wallet. "How much do we owe you for hauling?"

"Ten bucks will be fine, and I'll throw in a bale of hay," Smokey stated.

"Are you sure?" Rose asked.

Feeling a little uneasy, Smokey declared, "Ten dollars is all I will take. I should probably get going; I have a busy day tomorrow."

Shaking hands, John gave Smokey the ten-dollar

bill. Smokey set fresh hay on top of the old, unusable bales in the aisle of the barn.

Smokey walked over to Laura, patted her on the head, and said, "Take care of that rain rot. Good luck with her, kid."

Much to his surprise, Smokey felt a warm rush as Laura's little arms wrapped around his plump middle.

"Thanks, again Smokey—" Pop-Pop began, but Smokey waved him off.

"Yeah, well, gotta go," he said, scurrying to his rig. He jumped in and drove toward the house to turn the trailer around. As he passed Pop-Pop's family waving goodbye to him, Smokey couldn't hide the smile that covered his face. It had been a while since Smokey felt a part of something this meaningful and important.

"Come on, Laura," Mom-Mom said. "Let's put Sugar in the barn. We need to get both of you to bed. Tomorrow morning we need to start working on the rain rot, and Sugar sure needs a good grooming."

Laura carefully led Sugar into the barn, making sure she found her a bucket of water.

Pop-Pop brought in two small flakes of the fresh, soft hay Smokey had left for her. He placed the hay in the corner of the stall, next to her water bucket.

Sugar lowered her head and dragged Laura over to the tasty hay. The pony quickly grabbed a mouthful and began chewing in delight, closing her eyes and savoring every strand.

"I think it's been some time since she's had decent hay," Rose stated.

"Pop-Pop, can she have more?" Laura asked.

"No. Too much rich hay could make her sick."

Laura took the pony's halter off and went to stand with her parents, as they watched Sugar peacefully eating.

"I made an apple pie earlier today," Mom-Mom announced. "Who would like a slice?"

"That sounds wonderful," Rose replied.

Laura went over to Sugar and whispered in her ear, "See you in the morning. I love you, Sugar."

Laura headed out of the stall as Pop-Pop secured the door and turned out the lights. John challenged his daughter, "Laura, race you to the house?"

Laura nodded and immediately darted up the driveway.

Watching Laura and her dad race to the house, Mom-Mom nostalgically remembered how Pop-Pop and Rose used to do the same when Rose was Laura's age.

"We need to get home," Rose said. "John is ushering at church in the morning."

"Mom, Dad, may I spend the night at Mom-

Mom's?" Laura pleaded. "I need to make sure that Sugar is doing all right in the morning."

Pop-Pop assured Laura's parents, "We can get up early and meet you at church."

"Of course," John answered. "Your mother brought church clothes for you just in case you were late coming home."

"We have to get up around 6 a.m. Sugar is going to need a lot of attention. I can remember, about twenty years ago, a horse that was covered with rain rot like Sugar. It took nearly three months to get him healthy," said Pop-Pop.

After Laura finished her dessert, her parents headed home. Laura went upstairs and took a long hot shower.

Pop-Pop came upstairs to say goodnight to her. She climbed into the tightly fitted sheets and Pop-Pop tucked the handmade quilt over her.

"Are you tired, sweetheart?" Pop-Pop asked. "You're awfully quiet."

"No, I'm just worried about Sugar," Laura confessed.

"She'll be okay. It may take a little time, but we'll get her all fixed up." Pop-Pop smiled.

"I really wanted to start riding her..." Laura trailed off, biting back tears.

"Laura, we don't know if she is even broke to ride,"

Pop-Pop explained. "You need to get some sleep, young lady. We can worry about this tomorrow. I love you. Goodnight."

Pop-Pop kissed her on the forehead and whispered, "You're the reason Sugar is in the barn tonight." As he headed downstairs, Pop-Pop had a new bounce in his step.

Laura lay in bed fretting and thinking to herself, *I hope I can ride her soon! I really want to go to the State Fair with her and win the trophy!*

CHAPTER TEN

M om-Mom was the first one up Sunday morning, even before the sun rose.

She came down the steps very quietly, trying not to wake Laura or Pop-Pop. She made her way to the kitchen and clicked on the coffee maker. While her beloved coffee brewed, she began to peel potatoes for breakfast. Mom-Mom's home fries were Laura's favorite part of the morning meal. Mom-Mom placed the freshly-peeled potatoes in her lime-green bowl and added some cold water. Then, with much anticipation, she poured herself a cup of fresh coffee and sat at the antique kitchen table under the bay window. Mom-Mom watched the sun rise. There was enough light to see the silhouette of the barn.

Mom-Mom stood up quietly from the table and set

her coffee carefully on the kitchen counter. She began to collect the supplies they would need to take care of Sugar's rain rot. She placed the baby oil and Listerine on the mahogany stool by the kitchen door.

Just then, Laura entered the room, startling Mom-Mom. "Good morning, Mom-Mom," she said as she stretched her still-sleepy arms.

"You sure are up early, young lady. Are you anxious to see your new friend in the barn? I hope Sugar is okay. Ponies don't do well living by themselves.

"May I go check on Sugar *before* breakfast?" Laura begged.

"Of course, but first go upstairs and get dressed, and wake up Pop-Pop," Mom-Mom insisted.

"Yes, ma'am!" Laura turned and flew up the stairs.

"Is the house on fire?" Pop-Pop joked as he met her near the top.

"Mom-Mom said I could go down to the barn to see Sugar!"

"You better slow down a little," he suggested. "I'll meet you downstairs." The smell of simmering bacon led him to the kitchen.

"I think you're the best cook on the East Coast, and I was smart enough to marry you," Pop-Pop bragged, as he wrapped his arms around Mom-Mom.

"You have always been a charmer," Mom-Mom chuckled. "I have everything you need for Sugar on the stool by the door. Take them down to the barn. Try to rub her down with the baby oil; that will loosen up the scabs and make it easier to pick them off. Then we will use the Listerine to clean up Sugar's skin."

Just then, Laura ran back into the kitchen. "I'm ready!" she declared excitedly.

"Get your boots on, young lady, and we will go see how Sugar did last night," Pop-Pop said, smiling.

"Don't be long," Mom-Mom fussed. "We need to eat breakfast and get to church on time."

Pop-Pop and Laura went to the barn. Pop-Pop gently tugged on Laura's long ponytail and commanded, "Whoa, Pony!" Laura looked up at Pop-Pop, and the two began to laugh.

They walked into the dark, lonely barn. When Sugar heard them, she started to nicker. She seemed very happy to have company. Sugar met Laura and Pop-Pop enthusiastically at the opening of the stall door.

"She's feeling better!" Pop-Pop observed.

Sugar, in her excitement to see her owners and to get out the door, almost ran over Laura. Laura smacked Sugar on the shoulder and held her ground. "No, Sugar!" she scolded. "You need to wait!"

Sugar quickly backed up and stood quietly in the stall.

"Well done, Laura," Pop-Pop said. "That's just the

way to be the boss. You can tell that Sugar knows better. Someone has taught her manners in the past. It's very important that she respects you."

"Good girl, Sugar," Laura said, as she patted the pony's neck.

"We better rub her down with the baby oil and get up to the house for breakfast. When we get home from church, you can take her out for a walk and let her graze for a while," Pop-Pop explained.

"Can I rub it on?" Laura asked.

"Sure. Here you go." Pop-Pop handed her the oil.

"Should I pour it on or put it in my hand?

"Just put it in the palm of your hand and start near her withers, working your way down. Don't get right behind her; stay on her side so you don't get kicked," Pop-Pop instructed.

"Is this good?" Laura asked as she began to spread the oil on Sugar's loose winter coat.

"That's perfect!" Pop-Pop chuckled as Laura became covered in pony hair. "It looks like we have two ponies now!"

"This is messy!" Laura said, trying to get the hair out of her mouth. "I'm going to have to take a bath before church."

It took almost half of the bottle to cover the rain rot. When they were finished, they swiftly headed for the house.

After church, Mom-Mom, Pop-Pop, and Laura went to the barn to continue treating the fungus. As Mom-Mom picked the large chunks of scabs, Sugar's raw skin underneath began to bleed. With every tug, Sugar pinned her ears and scooted away from Mom-Mom to avoid the pain.

"This is worse than I thought," Mom-Mom sighed. "She may need a vet and antibiotics."

"Will she be okay?" Laura asked with concern.

"She should be fine," Mom-Mom answered. "It's just going to take some time for her to heal, and the medicine will make sure it doesn't get any worse."

Laura thought to herself, *I hope Sugar heals soon; I can't wait to start riding her.*

"I will call Dr. Hall in the morning," Pop-Pop promised. "It's been a while since I've seen him." He put his arm around Laura. "Your grandmother is a wonderful nurse."

With a chuckle in her voice, Mom-Mom clarified, "I don't know about that, but I think Sugar has had enough of me picking the rain rot for today. Laura, let's take her out for some grass."

Laura led Sugar to the lush, green meadow across the driveway from the barn. When Sugar saw the thick, green grass, she lowered her head and made a beeline, dragging Laura with her. When they reached the mouth-watering meadow, Sugar immediately dropped her head and ate.

"They look content," Mom-Mom said to Pop-Pop, as they watched Laura and Sugar. Pop-Pop smiled in agreement.

"When the vet comes, he should worm her. She looks like she has a wormy belly. I know she's sweet, but I hope we can get her straightened out," Mom-Mom said with concern.

"I noticed her big belly, too. It looked worse after Laura groomed her. You can see more of her under all the hair. It could take a couple of months to get her healthy," Pop-Pop said.

"Jack, I understand why you bought her, but this may not be the best pony for Laura. She's obviously been neglected. Who knows if she's even broke to ride? Let's see what the vet says and how much the bill will be for him. Maybe, if Rags or Pinocchio is available, we can still get one of them and then decide what to do with Sugar," Mom-Mom said in frustration.

"I know that Rags is ideal for her, but I have a feeling Sugar is the right pony. There's just something special about her. She has the kindest eyes I've ever seen. Trust me, everything is going to work out," Pop-Pop declared.

He motioned for Laura to bring Sugar back to the barn. "I'm going to walk around the pasture to check the fence with Laura, and then we can turn Sugar out. John's going to help me repair any fence when they come to pick up Laura."

"I hope you are right," Mom-Mom said, as she headed up the driveway. "I'll be in the garden if you need anything."

"Is Mom-Mom upset?" Laura asked as she put Sugar in the stall.

"Maybe a little. She's just worried and wants to make sure Sugar is the right pony for you. Let's not think about that now. We need to walk the fence line to make sure it's safe."

"Yes, sir. What should I do?"

"Follow me; look for nails sticking out on the boards. We don't want her to get cut by a nail. Then we will walk to the pasture and check for gopher holes. She could accidentally step in one and break a leg."

With a hammer and nails, Pop-Pop and Laura walked the entire field, fixing half a dozen boards. Laura walked the field from one end to the other, looking for any holes.

"I think that will do it," Pop-Pop said. "I think we can turn her out. Did you find any problems?"

"No, just found a couple of big rocks. I threw them under the fence. Should I go get her?"

"Yes, let's turn her out for a couple of hours. Before you let her go, walk her around the fence line so she sees everything. I don't want her to be excited to be out and run into something," Pop-Pop instructed.

Laura led Sugar around the entire two-acre pasture. The small stream that divided the field was deeper than usual and Laura found rocks to step on to cross without getting wet. Sugar was hesitant to follow and planted her feet, refusing to get them wet. Laura tried to coax Sugar and then pulled her with all her weight. Without any warning, Sugar leaped into the air, jumping the stream as if it was a three-foot jump.

She landed on the other side and looked back at Laura, who was lying on the ground covered in mud from head to toe.

"Are you okay?" Pop-Pop asked as he ran over to check on Laura.

"Yes, I'm fine. Just a little dirty," Laura replied as she sat up and started to brush herself off. Sugar walked over to Laura, pushing her with her nose.

"I think she's sorry," Pop-Pop snickered. "She's seen the whole field; go ahead and let her off the shank. We need to get you cleaned up before your parents arrive."

Laura released the snap under the halter and let Sugar free. They headed to the gate with Sugar following close behind. She watched them pass through the gate as they walked away from her and she started to whinny.

"I don't think Sugar likes being alone," Pop-Pop said as he looked back at the pony.

"I know, I wouldn't want to be alone," Laura said as she slowly walked in her heavy mud-spattered jeans. "Can we get her a friend?"

"Let's wait and see what the vet says."

The following Monday morning, Pop-Pop and Mom-Mom were finishing breakfast and enjoying their coffee, when the phone rang.

"Hello," Pop-Pop answered.

"Hi, this is Lisa from Dr. Hall's office returning your call about a Shetland pony," the receptionist stated. "Dr. Hall can see her at 4 p.m. today."

"That's perfect," Pop-Pop replied. "Thanks for your call." Pop-Pop hung up the phone and called Rose to let her know the time.

Laura and her mom arrived at Pop-Pop's at 3:45 p.m., not wanting to miss Dr. Hall. Pop-Pop had Sugar out eating grass. Laura jumped out of the car as soon as her mom parked.

"How's she doing?" Laura asked. "Hi, Sugar; I missed you."

"I'm doing fine, too, thanks for asking," Pop-Pop joked.

Just then, a substantial green truck with a white vet box in the back pulled into the driveway. When the truck stopped, a very tall, rugged-looking man stepped out.

Laura thought to herself, *That's the tallest person I have ever seen!*

"Jack Anderson, it sure is nice to see you," Dr. Hall stated. "That is the cutest pony I have seen in a long time."

Pop-Pop motioned to Laura to bring Sugar back to the barn.

"Thanks for fitting us in today," Pop-Pop said. As the men shook hands, Pop-Pop continued, "Sure is nice to see you, too."

Laura led Sugar back to the barn. The two men caught up on old times as Dr. Hall got supplies out of his truck.

"Lisa didn't tell me what you needed today for the pony," Dr. Hall said. "By the looks of her, you're going to need to know when the baby is due."

"Uh... no..." Pop-Pop started. "I thought she had a bad case of worms, but now that you mention it, she does look pregnant!"

CHAPTER ELEVEN

D r. Hall finished his initial exam of Sugar and went out to his truck to get the antibiotics.

"Laura, I'll be right back," Pop-Pop said. "Start trying to comb out her mane with that blue comb in the bucket. I'm going to pay Dr. Hall and get her medicine."

"Here is Sulfa Trim for the fungus. Give her five, twice a day for ten days. I will recheck her then and see how she's doing," Dr. Hall instructed. "I didn't want to say anything in front of Laura, but she's in foal. She's already started to bag up. I think she's going to foal within the next month or so. It's hard to tell because she's underweight, but I would keep a close eye on her."

"Do you think she'll be okay?" Pop-Pop asked.

"I hope so, but I'm concerned. I don't like how thin she is, and with time at the auction, she could have been exposed to strangles or shipping fever. The next ten days will show if she picked up anything. Keep a close eye on her and take her temperature every day. Call me if you see a runny nose, cough, or if she stops eating. Keep the rain rot clean and put Desitin on it, and that will help keep it from getting re-infected. I think, with diligence and keeping a close eye on her, we might be okay."

"I sure hope she's okay. I haven't been to a sale in a long time; I didn't think about her getting sick," Pop-Pop said, as he watched Dr. Hall write the bill. "What about the foal?"

"If she doesn't get a fever, the foal should be fine. Hopefully, she wasn't bred with anything too large. It's hard to know how big the foal will be or if she'll have trouble with the delivery. Call me if she starts to foal. I would feel better being here in case she gets into trouble." Dr. Hall handed Jack the bill. "You can mail the check to the office. Do you have any questions? I'm not trying to scare you, but I'm a bit worried about her."

"No, I don't have any questions now. I would hate to see something happen to her as attached as Laura has become to her. I guess I shouldn't have bought the pony," Pop-Pop said, leaning on the truck with his hand over his face.

"I understand, but I know if anybody can help her, it's your wife. She's one of the best caregivers I have ever seen. You could get Laura another pony so that she has something to ride. It could be quite a while before Sugar can be ridden."

Pop-Pop nodded in resignation. "We *did* find her the perfect pony, but Laura changed her mind on wanting him. Now with buying Sugar, we may not have enough money to buy him even if we could get him again."

"Why don't you call Mrs. Taylor and explain about Sugar? She may have some history about where she was and who she was bred with. Don't worry about my bill now. We can always work that out later. I would rather Laura have that pony first. You were always good to me, and I missed seeing you after you sold out," Dr. Hall explained. "Well, gotta go, or I'll be late for my next appointment."

Pop-Pop made his way back into the barn and heard Laura talking to Sugar as she combed her thick mane.

"Laura, I have her medicine. I'm going to go to the house to get some applesauce to mix with it."

"Why do you need applesauce?" Laura asked.

"It's an old trick to get Sugar to eat her medicine without her knowing. I'll dissolve the pills in water and then mix them with applesauce. Sugar will think she's getting a treat!"

"You are so smart!" Laura declared.

"Thank you, but I'm not sure about that," Pop-Pop joked. "I'll be right back."

Pop-Pop walked into the kitchen where Mom-Mom and Rose were snapping fresh green beans.

Rose looked up. "What did Dr. Hall say?"

Pop-Pop walked over to the table and sat down across from them. He scratched his head and with a long pause said, "Well, it looks like we will be having two ponies soon. She's in foal, and he thinks she could foal within a month."

The ladies looked at each other and began to laugh in delight. "That's exciting! Did you tell Laura?" Mom-Mom asked.

"No, I want to call Mrs. Taylor first and see if I can find out a little bit more about her."

"Mrs. Taylor left a message on the answering machine today. I must have been in the garden. She said Rags is still available if we want him," Mom-Mom said.

Pop-Pop sighed, "I think I made a mistake buying Sugar. Dr. Hall is worried about her. The fungus is going to take a while to clear up and she could have been exposed to shipping fever at the sale. Hopefully, the foal will be okay. It could be a long time until she can be ridden."

"Dad, I think she'll be okay. Buying Sugar wasn't a mistake. We can all pitch in and get her fixed up. Don't be so hard on yourself!"

"Thanks, Rose. That means a lot," Pop-Pop said as he held her hand. "I'm going to go call Mrs. Taylor. Where are the papers from the sale, Virginia? I haven't had a chance to go through them yet."

"They're right next to your chair, in a folder," Mom-Mom said.

Pop-Pop opened the folder and began to shuffle through the papers. He saw her American Shetland Pony Association registration papers and then the Coggins test that is required by the state to check for a mosquito-transmitted disease called EIA. He put all those papers to one side and then found what he was looking for: a small slip of paper. It was a stallion certificate stating that Sugar had been bred to Hadley Zeon.

"Look at this!" Pop-Pop exclaimed as he walked into the kitchen waving the paper, "Sugar was bred with one of Mrs. Taylor's finest stallions. This foal could be really nice. I'm going to call her now."

He quickly made his way into the living room, plunked himself down in his chair, and picked up the phone.

"Mrs. Taylor, it's Jack Anderson."

"Oh, good. I left you a message earlier today. Jodi is going to ride Pinocchio at the fair. If you still want Rags, he's yours."

"Well, I'm not sure. I took Laura to the auction this weekend, looking for a saddle, and we bought a pony—"

Mrs. Taylor interrupted, "I'm surprised you would buy a pony from a sale. You know everyone just unloads the bad or sick ones there."

"I know, but this pony was special. She's a Hadley pony. Her registered name is Hadley Spider. The dealer who had her said the owner had died and her niece didn't know what to do with her."

"Oh my goodness. I had no idea that Mrs. White died. She bought Spider from me as a foal. She's one of the nicest ponies I've ever bred. I had her here all last summer. I used her for camps and bred her to Zeon. Is she in foal?"

"Yes, just had the vet here. She's covered in rain rot, thin, and looks like she could foal in the next month or so."

"That poor thing; she is so sweet. I can't thank you enough for getting her from the sale. Would you want to trade her for Rags? Jodi, my granddaughter, has always wanted her since she broke her. I would love to give her to Jodi. I would never let Jodi keep a gelding because they can't have babies," Mrs. Taylor chuckled.

"Really, are you sure?" Pop-Pop hesitated. "She's in rough shape."

"Yes, I would love to have her back. Do you want me to bring Rags down in the morning and I can pick her up?"

"That would be great! I can't wait to tell Laura! Thanks so much. I'll see you in the morning." Pop-Pop smiled as he hung up the phone.

Pop-Pop hustled into the kitchen, grabbed the applesauce, and started out the door, without divulging any information to Mom-Mom or Rose.

"Jack, Jack!" Mom-Mom said, "What did Mrs. Taylor say?"

Pop-Pop appeared startled. He stopped and leaned back in the doorway, "Sorry, I was so excited! Mrs. Taylor wants to trade Rags for Sugar. She's bringing him in the morning and picking up Sugar."

"What!?" Rose and Mom-Mom said at the same time.

"She wants Sugar back for her granddaughter, Jodi, and Laura can get Rags. This is perfect. We won't have to worry about Sugar's health, and Laura can go to the fair this year! I feel so relieved. I was so worried that I made a big mistake. It's all going to work out!" Pop-Pop exclaimed.

"Hold on, Jack Anderson! You are not the only one making the decisions around here. Laura loves that pony in the barn. Don't you think we should ask her what she wants? Mrs. Taylor is a very smart business-woman. She must know how nice Sugar is, and she doesn't give away *anything.* I think we need to have Laura's input on this, too!" Mom-Mom argued.

"I already told Mrs. Taylor to come in the morn-ing. I can't change my mind now. Laura will want Rags," Pop-Pop said, defending his decision.

"Dad, you will give Laura a choice. If there was a choice when Trigger got hurt, that he could live, but never be ridden again; I would never have wanted to get rid of him. He was more than just a pony to ride; he was my best friend. Laura knows in her heart who her best friend is going to be, and she needs to be the one to choose. Daddy, you're always trying to fix every-thing, like when you bought me another pony without asking me first. I needed time to cope with losing Trig-ger, and then I may have wanted a new pony, but you never asked me what I wanted. I know you meant well, but you can't protect us from getting hurt. I guess I'm a lot like you!" Rose said as she embraced her dad. "Let's go ask Laura what she wants."

"I'm sorry, Rose, I just wanted to stop you from hurting," Pop-Pop replied. "You're right about Laura.

Let's go see what she thinks. Will both of you come with me?"

As the threesome entered the barn, they could hear chattering coming from Sugar's stall. They stopped and listened to the conversation.

"Do you like your hair done this way?" Laura asked Sugar. "Tomorrow I'll bring my box of ribbon, so you can be extra beautiful."

"I'm back, Laura; sorry I took so long," Pop-Pop announced, not wanting to startle her. "I have the applesauce. She looks lovely! You have been hard at work on her."

"She does look gorgeous!" Mom-Mom said. "Pop-Pop talked to Mrs. Taylor about Sugar."

"What did she say?" Laura asked.

"Well, she said that she would like to have Sugar back," Pop-Pop answered. "I didn't tell you, earlier, but Sugar is going to have a foal. Dr. Hall thinks in the next month she will foal."

"A baby? Oh my gosh! I'm so excited," Laura exclaimed.

"I know having a foal would be exciting, but it can be risky. She could have some problems foaling and the vet is concerned about her health. She could be sick from being at the auction, and he thinks it could be a while before you can ride her," Mom-Mom explained.

"The good news is she is broke and has been used for camps."

"I don't care about riding her. I will take care of her and the baby. She will be fine," Laura pleaded.

"Laura, I know you would, but Mrs. Taylor would be willing to trade Rags for Sugar. She would like to have Sugar for Jodi," Pop-Pop said. "You could go to the fair this year on Rags."

"Sweetie," Rose said as she sat on the hay in front of Laura. "It's your decision. Whatever you decide, we will support you. What pony do you want?"

Laura was speechless. She stared at Sugar as everyone waited to hear her decision, trying to be patient. Laura took a deep breath and said, "I love them both. When I rode Rags, it was awesome. I have thought about taking him to the fair since I rode him. Sugar needs me, and I love her, but I really want to ride. I don't know what to do."

"Laura, I want you to have a special pony like I had with Trigger. Who do you think could be your best friend?" Rose asked.

"Oh, that's easy. I know who that is," Laura said with much relief. "I've made my decision!"

CHAPTER TWELVE

"**W**hat time do you think Mrs. Taylor will be here?" Mom-Mom asked.

"Any minute," Pop-Pop said. "She was going to head over here once she finished her morning chores. I'm going down to the barn now. Are you coming?"

"Yes," Mom-Mom said. "I wouldn't miss it."

Just then, they heard the sound of Mrs. Taylor's diesel truck and the clanky stock trailer it hauled, slowing down and turning onto the driveway. The red truck's loud diesel engine roared as Mrs. Taylor steered it to a parking spot beside the barn. When she cut off the engine, the faint sound of a whinny came from the trailer. Sugar perked up and neighed when she heard it.

"Good morning, Jack and Virginia," Mrs. Taylor

said as she shook Pop-Pop's hand, "I have the pony for you. Can I see Spider before I unload?

"Sure, follow me," Pop-Pop said, as he headed into the barn and to Sugar's stall. "We have been calling her Sugar. Laura doesn't like spiders, so she can't bring herself to call her that."

"Sugar is a great name for her. She does look rough. It's so sad that she was neglected after Mrs. White died. Last year, in the middle of summer, she was stunning. Her coat shined like a new penny, and her dapples stood out like I have never seen before. Her mane, when it's washed, is pure white. Are you sure you won't change your mind?" Mrs. Taylor begged.

"No, Laura won't part with her. I appreciate your offer, and I'm sorry that I agreed to the trade before I talked to Laura," Pop-Pop explained. "Virginia has the money for Missy. I can't thank you enough for selling her to us. I know Sugar will love the company."

"Here you go, Mrs. Taylor," Mom-Mom said as she handed the money to Mrs. Taylor. "Two hundred and fifty dollars."

"Perfect. Here are her papers," Mrs. Taylor said, as she pulled the envelope out of her dress pocket. "She will be one on August 18th. Missy looks very weedy next to the other yearlings, but I think it's just because she's the youngest. We better get her off the trailer, so I can get back to the farm."

The wide door swung open and a very tiny pony looked back at them. Mrs. Taylor led her off the trailer. She leaped down onto the pavement, causing her to slip. "Be careful little one," Mrs. Taylor said to Missy.

"She's a beautiful chestnut. I love her cream-colored mane," Mom-Mom said.

"Here you go," Mrs. Taylor said as she handed Jack the lead rope. "Have fun with your new ponies. If you ever change your mind, I'll buy Sugar at any time. I can't tell you how much Jodi wants to own her. I bet you're going to have a spectacular foal. Call me when she has the baby. Well, got to go."

"Mrs. Taylor, we are very sorry about Jodi," Mom-Mom said. "I hope she understands."

"Trust me, I understand. Jodi has Rags for now." Mrs. Taylor smiled and climbed back into the truck.

Pop-Pop led the new and frightened pony into the barn as the trailer pulled away. He put her in the stall next to Sugar and let her have the freedom to explore her new world. Missy reached her tiny nose through the bars to meet her new companion.

"I wish Laura could be here," Mom-Mom said as she watched the ponies. "I love it when they seem like they are whispering to each other in pony nickering. I'm going to get Laura's room ready. She'll be out of school for the summer on Friday. I'm so excited that Rose and John agreed to let her stay with us until the foal is born."

"I am, too. It's going to be a great summer. Is Rose bringing her today to see Missy?"

"No, John is bringing her tonight. Rose has a church meeting."

"I'll wait till tonight to feed them, then. I'm going to turn Sugar and Missy out together for a while, and then clean the stalls."

"Do you need help?" Mom-Mom asked.

"No, I'm good," Pop-Pop said as he led the two ponies toward the pasture.

"Okay, I'll be up at the house," Mom-Mom said. She smiled and headed up the driveway.

Pop-Pop led the two ponies into the large meadow and turned them to face the gate. He let them go and leaned on the gate, putting one foot on the lower fence board. As he watched them walk away, it seemed as if they were glued together.

That evening, Laura came running into the barn to see the newest pony. "I just brought them in after being out all day," Pop-Pop said. "Here's Missy. Isn't she cute? She's petite for her age, but I think she will catch up with time."

Laura slowly entered the stall and carefully tried to touch the skittish yearling. Missy stretched her short neck toward Laura to investigate the newest person in her life.

"Where's the new boat?" John loudly joshed as he walked toward the stall, startling Missy and causing her to move away from Laura.

"Dad, you need to be careful around Missy," Laura instructed. "She's pretty nervous around new people. She's so tiny, but it looks like Sugar loves her."

"Sorry, didn't mean to scare her," John apologized. "She seems nice."

"It's okay, Dad," Laura said as she shut Missy's door and went into Sugar's stall. "I sure missed her today."

"She's doing great. She has no fever, and she is eating all the feed I give her." Pop-Pop sighed. "We should feed them dinner, and I think Mom-Mom will have dinner ready for us soon."

Laura started to mix Sugar's feed, as Pop-Pop prepared Missy's dinner. The two ponies whinnied with excitement, anxiously waiting for their dinners. As quickly as their meals were delivered, they were gone. Laura gave them each two flakes of hay while Pop-Pop brought them their water.

"Sugar's appetite is great," Pop-Pop said as they

walked to the house. "That's a good sign that she's not going to get sick."

The last day of the school year finally arrived, and Rose was the first in line to pick up her daughter.

"I thought the day would never end," Laura announced as she climbed into the front seat. "My friends want me to write them when Sugar has her baby. All of them gave their addresses before we left. Everyone was so nice today."

"I'm so happy to hear that," Rose said, as she drove toward her parents' farm. "How is your report card?"

"It was good: one A, three B's, and one C."

"Great job, Laura. Your dad is going to be very happy to hear that. I'm so proud of you!"

"Thanks, Mom. Did you bring my suitcase?"

"Yes. It's in the trunk. We sure are going to miss you. Hopefully, Sugar will have the baby soon."

"I'm going to miss you too, but I can't wait to spend the night in the barn."

"I hope your grandfather is up to it. He's not as young as he used to be," Rose said. "But I have to admit, I think the ponies are making him feel younger."

Laura reluctantly organized her temporary room at her grandparents' house, wishing she could stop and run down to the barn.

"Are you finished yet?" Pop-Pop hollered upstairs. "We need to feed the ponies."

"Almost," Laura said, as she put her last pair of shorts in the drawer.

"Jack, don't rush her," Mom-Mom fussed. "I told her I want that room to be kept nice and tidy."

"All done," Laura said, as she flew down the stairs. "I'm ready!"

At the barn, Pop-Pop and Laura only saw Missy standing. Sugar was nowhere in sight. They quickly began to search for her and found her lying flat and motionless under the large willow tree at the far end of the pasture.

"Come on girl, get up," Pop-Pop encouraged, trying to get her to her feet. "I don't think she feels very good. Laura, get her halter and shank."

"Is she okay?" Laura asked nervously.

"I'm not sure. Be careful that Missy doesn't get out when you open the gate and hurry!"

Laura ran as fast as she could, climbing the fence instead of opening the gate. She grabbed the halter and shank and made her way quickly back to Sugar, who had just stood up on her own.

"She's up. Let's get her into the barn," Pop-Pop urged. He led the weary pony to her stall. "Put Missy in her stall, and then bring me the thermometer," he said.

Pop-Pop carefully tied Sugar to the stall door and began to examine her as Laura looked on anxiously. He pressed his ear up to her belly, listening for gut sounds. Then he took her temperature. He flipped her upper lip and examined her gums, checking for good color. He peeked at her utter to see if milk was coming in.

"Her temperature is normal, and I can't find anything wrong with her," he said. He let Sugar go. "Go ahead and give her dinner, and hopefully, she'll eat it."

Laura quickly made up Sugar's dinner and served it. She put the grain in the feed tub and showed Sugar where it was. Missy whinnied for hers with much anticipation, but Sugar looked at her food and turned away, hiding in the corner.

"Do you think she's sick?" Laura asked.

"I'm not sure. I don't think she's colicky, which would be like a bad stomach ache. She has gut sounds, so I'm confident her stomach doesn't hurt. Her temperature is normal, so I don't think it's shipping fever. Her gums have good color, which is a good sign. Her utter isn't full, so she's not close to foaling yet," Pop-Pop explained. "I'm going to call Dr. Hall and get your grandmother. Can you watch her? If she lays down, don't let her roll, okay? I'll be a fast as I can."

"We will be fine, Pop-Pop," Laura said, as she stroked Sugar's neck.

Pop-Pop raced to the house and quietly said, "This is too stressful. I wish we would have traded for Rags."

"Do you have a headache, Sugar?" Laura asked as she combed through Sugar's mane with her fingers. "Look at Missy; she can't stop staring at you. She's worried, too! Let me get you an apple, it's from my lunch. I saved it for you. Take a bite, and I'll give some to Missy."

Sugar refused the apple and became restless. She kicked at her belly and looked at her sides.

I better go get Pop-Pop, Laura thought to herself. *But what if she rolls while I'm gone? I can't leave her!*

"Sugar, don't lie down, please," Laura pleaded, as she watched Sugar lie down anyway in the deep straw bed. "Okay, girl. Don't roll. Just lie still."

The distressed pony lay flat on her side and groaned in pain. She picked her head up, looked at her hindquarters, and then rested for a moment, only to repeat this several times.

Laura stayed close to Sugar's face, caressing it

when she was still. The sound of water pouring onto the straw confused Laura.

"I wish Pop-Pop was here," Laura said as she watched Sugar helplessly.

All of a sudden, Sugar lifted her head, and with the loudest groan, squeezed her belly. Out slid a tiny foal covered in a wet film. Sugar laid her head back down in exhaustion. The foal lay motionless.

"Sugar, you did it," Laura exclaimed. She got up to take a closer look at the foal.

The foal showed no signs of life. Laura looked on in despair. Missy watched the foal too and pawed at her stall door, trying to get a closer look.

Laura felt stressed with Missy banging on the wall and the foal not moving. She leaned down to examine the foal more closely. She realized its nose was covered by the sack it was born in. She couldn't breathe. Laura quickly removed the slimy cover from her nose and began to rub her. Suddenly, the foal stirred and, within a couple of seconds, became lively.

"You scared me, little one," Laura scolded the new life. "I'm glad you're okay. Sugar, look at your beautiful baby."

Sugar slowly stood up and turned around to meet her daughter. She licked her all over as the wobbly baby attempted to stand up.

"Laura, how is she doing?" Pop-Pop said, entering

the barn. "Dr. Hall is on his way." Pop-Pop and Mom-Mom peered into the stall and were shocked to see the foal.

"Sugar had her baby," Laura announced, proudly showing them the foal. "Isn't she beautiful? She didn't move at first, but then I took that yucky stuff off her nose, and she was fine."

"Unbelievable," Mom-Mom said. "You delivered your first foal by yourself. Laura, I'm so proud of you! You're an amazing little girl."

"You did a great job," Pop-Pop added. He went into the stall to get a closer look at the new addition. "Let me take a look at you, little one. It's a girl and look at those markings. She's a pinto, with four white stockings and a wide blaze. I think she's going to be chestnut and white. She's perfect; I couldn't be happier with her. I'm so proud of you. Were you scared?"

"I was terrified. I couldn't move at first," Laura explained. "But then Missy started banging her stall, and that's when I realized I needed to wipe her nose off. I think Missy may have helped me save her."

"She must have known you needed help," Mom-Mom said, putting her hand through the bars to scratch Missy's nose. "She's a keeper, for sure! I'm going to go call your parents and tell them the exciting news."

Within an hour, Dr. Hall, Rose, and John arrived to

see the baby. Everyone watched Sugar and her baby
get to know each other. The little one leaped in the air
out of pure excitement. She had learned to use her legs
and wanted everyone to see her many talents.

"Sugar certainly tricked us, but she has plenty of
milk. That's one athletic foal. I think she's pretty
special," Dr. Hall observed. "What are you going to
name her?"

All the adults looked at Laura, waiting to hear if
she had a name for the baby she'd saved."I'm going to
name her Hip Hop!" Laura giggled.

"I love it, Laura!" Mom-Mom smiled.

"This is way better than winning the trophy at the
State Fair!" Laura announced, turning to look at them
all. "This is the best day of my life!"

GET BOOK 2 IN THE HIP HOP TALES SERIES:

A BIT OF MAELSTROM

Laura Maynor is loving life at Hadley Farm, spending time with Sugar, Sugar's yearling daughter, Hip Hop, and her best friend Jodi. One day, a wild mustang arrives at the farm capturing Laura's heart. Unfortunately, the mustang's trainer bullies him, much like Laura was bullied at school.

Laura finds her way through the spider web of challenges in front of her and works tirelessly to save the mustang she's named Maelstrom. Now she has to face the repercussions of her choices and will be confronted with life-changing decisions to save him.

ABOUT THE AUTHOR

Deborah was born in rural Harford County in 1970. Her love and passion for horses were fostered at a very young age by her beloved grandfather. She spent countless hours following him everywhere, learning everything and anything she could about horses.

By her late teens, Deborah was teaching younger children how to ride while competing in national-level events. She's now focused on writing and educating young riders through her books, expanding her own horse education, and enjoying her family.

Made in the USA
Middletown, DE
01 July 2022

68232550R00071